Abraham Lincoln for the Defense

ISBN -13: **9781493767090**

Warren Bull, Publisher

Other books by Warren Bull: Death in the Moonlight, Murder
Manhattan Style, Heartland, Killer Eulogy and Other Stories

To My Family and Friends

Chapter One

April 6, 1868 Springfield, Illinois

My dearest darling niece, Eppie:

You asked me about a painful time. And I after much prayerful thought I decided that I could and should answer. Yes, I did know Mr. Lincoln personally. Yes, he did me a great service (or two, or even more.) Yes, there are still mysteries, which no one can unravel. For who can read the human heart? If you read what happened in a book you would think the author had painted himself into a corner and then had to track through the wet paint to escape.

I will ask your indulgence as to how I will reply. My memories of Mr. Lincoln start with when I learned of his death not so very long ago.

I did not know until then that my heart could once again contain such grief or that my eyes could again cry such bitter salt tears. We were all of us finally coming out of the nightmare of the war years, passing on to the rest of our lives but not forgetting our valiant dead. We were just beginning to see the sun peek through the clouds of extended darkness when the news of the assassination of Mr. Lincoln once again flung us into the pit of despair. The whole town and the countryside around went into dark mourning. Black was the only color to be worn and even the crows in the trees seemed to be grieving. With the passing of the seasons it seems that life has slowly seeped back into the town and finally even into me.

There is no one here whose life was not touched by that man so curiously ugly that he seemed almost beautiful. Even strangers and newcomers claim an acquaintance with the martyred president now. Stories about him grow and change with each new day. I cannot think that Mr. Lincoln would be other than pleased with that since he himself would change his stories to the temper of his audience. I have, myself, heard Mr. Lincoln tell of his wrestling match with Jack Armstrong so that Mr. Armstrong won, that Mr. Lincoln won, and that the outcome was never clearly settled depending on who was listening and the effect Mr. Lincoln wanted at the moment.

Even so, dear niece Eppie, I want to tell you about the time when Mr. Lincoln came into my life and set it on a course that I could not have imagined. The strange events of that time came to a conclusion that was even stranger than the events themselves. I still scarcely know what to think about it all. I did not know all back then that I will tell you now. When I moved to Springfield afterward I started collecting scraps of the truth one bit at a time. Over the next months and even years I slowly pieced them together like piecing a crazy quilt until I had as much of the truth as anyone under heaven could know. I have held it to myself and to my dear husband (who has relentlessly tracked parts of the story back to their lair on his own and who gathered pieces in places where I dared not tread.) Very little escapes my husband when he puts his mind and his efforts to find it. This search between the two of us has brought us closer together. He knows and supports my telling you. I find I am excited about the idea of sharing what I know with you and through you to our descendants.

Yours forever,

Aunt Cassandra

P.S. I think it might help you if I tell you about some of the people involved as they were back then. I will list them for you as if this was a playbill or a novel.

Abraham Lincoln: An unmarried 32-year-old self-taught attorney and a member of the Illinois State Assembly. Although he lacked polish and self-confidence and was subject to fits of melancholy, he was seen as an up and coming young man who might even some day be elected to congress. Surprisingly to many people he became engaged to Mary Todd, one of the most sophisticated and eligible of the young women in town but the engagement was called off with no explanation. Then tongues did wag! He was retained as co-counsel for William, Arch and Henry Trailor who were accused of murdering Archibald Fisher.

Archibald Fisher: An unmarried man more than fifty years old with no set address and few visible possessions, but reputed wealth. His disappearance set events in motion.

William Trailor: A widowed farmer from Warren County, Illinois who was accused with his brothers of murdering Archibald Fisher.

Cassandra Trailor: Youngest daughter of William Trailor. She was a spinster although she was not entirely unattractive. (I know you are smiling at that.)

Daniel Trailor: Youngest son of William Trailor

Enoch Trailor: Second youngest son of William Trailor

3

Arch Trailor: An unmarried carpenter living in Springfield and brother of William and Henry who was accused with his brothers of murdering Archibald Fisher. He boarded permanently with his partner, Dutch Myers, and his partner's family.

Henry Trailor: A farmer with a wife and two children living in Clary's Grove who was accused of murdering Archibald Fisher with his brothers.

Hattie Trailor: Wife of Henry Trailor.

Adam Trailor: Son of Henry Trailor.

Abigail Trailor: Infant daughter of Henry Trailor.

"Dutch" Myers: A German immigrant who was Arch Trailor's partner in the carpentry business. He was a big man with a big heart. With his family he took boarders into his home. Archibald Fisher, William Trailor, and Henry Trailor were temporary boarders in his home when the strange events unfolded.

Elise Myers: The wife of Dutch Myers. She was kindly, smart, brave and pretty.

Israel Myers: The son of Dutch and Elise Myers.

George Washington Turner: Also known as G.W. A free black man who worked for Dutch Myers and Arch Trailor.

Samuel Franklin: A clerk at the Illinois Hotel and a permanent boarder at Myers.

Dennis Kelly: A traveling whiskey seller who boarded at Myers when he was in Springfield.

James Dorman: A newspaperman at the Sangamo Journal and a permanent boarder at Myers.

Leonard James: A blacksmith and a permanent boarder at Myers.

Elijah Hart: A small but strong drayman who ate his meals at Myers.

Nellie Caldwell: A young woman hired to help Mrs. Myers who lived at Myers.

Mary Todd: An unmarried woman who was one of the brightest lights in Springfield society. She was well educated, well read and interested in state politics which, of course, did not matter at all to her marital prospects. She was witty and pretty which made her "a catch." More important to many of her suitors, she came from a socially prominent family and was in position to inherit land and slaves from her father. Unexpectedly to many, she became engaged to Abraham Lincoln but the engagement was called off with no explanation, which resulted in no end of gossip and speculation in Springfield.

Stephen T. Logan: A former judge and the current law partner of Abraham Lincoln. With Edward D. Baker he was Lincoln's co-counsel during the Trailor murder trial.

Edward D. Baker: A British born lawyer who was a noted Whig orator. With Stephen T. Logan he was Lincoln's co-counsel during the Trailor murder trial.

David Davis: A circuit court judge.

Leonard Swett: An attorney formerly from Maine.

Jack Armstrong: A friend of Abraham Lincoln since his early adulthood. As young men, they had a wrestling match that has become a local legend.

Hannah Armstrong: Wife to Jack Armstrong and long time friend of Abraham Lincoln

Jim Maxey: A deputy. A man devoted to his duty as he found it.

Alonzo Wickersham: A deputy.

Caleb Young: The sheriff of Springfield. He faced an upcoming re-election.

Josiah Lamborn: Attorney General of the state of Illinois and prosecutor in the Trailor murder case.

Alvan Martin: The mayor of Springfield.

Asher Keys: Postmaster and tavern owner in Springfield.

Daniel May: One of the two judges in the Trailor murder case.

Zedekiah Lavely: One of the two judges in the Trailor murder case.

George Digby: Neighbor to William Trailor in Warren County and witness at his trial.

Increase Weaver: A minister in William Trailor's Methodist church.

Mildred Goodwin: A widow in Warren County.

Alexander Baldwin: Postmaster in Warren County, tavern owner and a witness in the trial

Edwin Brown: A bartender in Keys' tavern in Springfield. He hoped to keep his job.

Manasseh Porter: A citizen of Springfield. A hostler at a livery stable

Ignatius Langford: A citizen of Springfield. A mason who worked with Arch Trailor.

Edmund Hitchcock: The owner of the mill on spring creek.

"Pap" Douglas: The jailer in Springfield.

Asa Gilmore: A doctor in Warren County

Chapter Two

Twenty-seven years earlier

Monday, May 31, 1841, Springfield, Illinois

Close to noon, three men rode up the dusty main street of Springfield, Illinois for a friendly visit. But only two men rode out of town toward their homes the next day.

Riding in a one-horse carriage called a dearborn, were Archibald Fisher and William Trailor. Riding on a horse was Henry Trailor. Archibald Fisher was a thin, wiry man who looked much older than his fifty years. His black hair was streaked with white. There were lines etched deeply around his eyes and mouth. His forehead was wrinkled. Fisher was dressed in old, and often mended, but clean homespun work clothes. He sat stiffly bouncing like a sack of grain when the carriage jolted over ruts and holes in the dusty road. Fisher stared straight ahead ignoring the sights of the city. There was little animation in his flat brown eyes. Perhaps the most striking aspect of Fisher's appearance was that over his right eye three white scars extended into his hairline forming a rough N.

William Trailor was a strong, solidly built man in his forties with ruddy weathered features and callused, capable hands. His copper colored hair showed patches of white at the temples. William's pale green eyes moved alertly taking in the sights while he was keeping watch on his horse and the traffic surrounding him. He was dressed in clean sturdy homespun clothes. William held the reins with practiced ease and efficiency as he guided the gray mare through the heavily traveled street. He rode easily in the wagon automatically cushioning himself against the jolts and shaking of the carriage with his strong back and legs.

Henry Trailor looked like a younger, smaller and more energetic version of his older brother. His hair was more blond than red. Henry's features were more refined than William's were. With his jade colored eyes, his slim, strong body and his attention to his appearance most women found him handsome. Henry's clothing was obviously from a store. He rode a tall roan with white stockings on the front legs. The horse seemed a bit skittish. Henry controlled the animal and kept his saddle well.

Henry was pleased that his unflappable older brother, William, seemed impressed by the vigor and activity of Springfield. It felt good, strange but good, to think that Henry knew more about something than the older brother who had been like a father to him. William had been respectful toward his pretty wife, Hattie, his son, Adam, and the new baby girl, Abigail. He treated Henry more like an adult and less like a child than at any time in Henry's life. It was a heady feeling. William offered no criticism of Henry's drinking and "tom catting around" as he had so many times before. William did not tell Henry to "find a furrow and plow it," i.e. to find a job and stick with it. William did not even ask Henry if he were attending church. William seemed pleased with the work Henry and Hattie had done on the farm. Now Henry was leading the way, and pointing out sights of interest in a town he knew and his older brother did not.

William was proud of Henry even if he did not entirely like the experience of relying on another person instead of himself. William hoped Henry's wife and children would encourage Henry to finally become the responsible adult he had shown signs of becoming without ever quite fully developing into. He hoped that eventually Henry's wife could convince him to start attending church with her.

9

The men rode past buildings under construction. They saw heavy low wagons, called drays, hauling lumber and supplies, wagons with farm families who gawked at the activities around them, fine carriages pulled by matched teams of horses, and riders of many descriptions. The few wooden sidewalks teemed with drummers offering their wares for sale to people passing by and smiling merchants inviting people to enter their stores. Servants scurried, or tarried, on their errands carrying lists or packages. Neatly dressed men with soft clean hands escorted fashionably dressed women. In the gutters, scruffy dogs chased each other, while pigs rooted through garbage looking for food. Yelling boys contended with the animals for space as they pretended to be soldiers or Indians.

The taverns bustled despite the early hour. The churches stood in silence, as if resting after Sunday services. The men passed livery stables and doctors' offices. Henry led the older men past the rudimentary county and state offices. He led them by the architectural pride of the town, "Hoffman's Row." Hoffman's Row consisted of six two-story brick buildings on west Fifth Street. The men passed lawyers' offices and the small store formerly rented out for use as a courthouse. William admitted that he had never seen so many fine buildings in a row. The men ignored two boys fighting earnestly in a ditch by the side of the road. Finally, Henry directed his horse toward the home and business of "Dutch" Myers.

Before the dearborn was out of sight, Abraham Lincoln came out of one of the brick buildings and looked over at the boys.

"Will! Josh! Get out of the ditch and come over here."

The two boys reluctantly and slowly moved over to Lincoln with their heads hanging.

Lincoln stood towering over the boys and with his hands clasped behind him.

"Now what is this all about?" asked Lincoln.

Will eyed Josh angrily. "He's a thief!"

"You're a liar!" countered Josh.

"Those are harsh accusations," said Lincoln. "Especially between friends. No doubt if you're willing to make them you can back them up. Do you plan to stomp each other into bloody pudding? Maybe one of you should get a stick. Then the other one could get a rock. Then one of you could get a knife. And the other one could get a sword. Then one of you could get a rifle. And the other one could get a cannon. You could have a war. Is that what you want?"

Both boys said they did not.

"Maybe you need a little adjudication then."

"Would it hurt?" asked Josh.

"Only a little bit," said Lincoln, smiling. "What I mean is you could find an honest man to listen to both of you and judge your dispute. You'd each have a chance to present your side of the case and to answer questions posed to you then the judge would propose a solution that each of you would agree ahead of time to accept."

"Would you be the judge?" asked Will.

"I would accept whatever you decide," said Josh.

Lincoln stroked his chin and looked thoughtful for a few moments.

"Gentlemen I am appreciative of the honor you bestow and I will strive to be worthy of the responsibility. Will, you go first. Make an opening statement that summarizes your position."

"I found a cent last week. Then I lost it. Josh found it. He won't give it back to me."

"Succinct, well organized and precise. Will, you did an excellent job. Josh, its your turn."

"I found a cent today. It ain't the one Josh lost so I'm gonna keep her."

"Very well stated. Terse, but not taciturn. Complete in every particular. I commend you gentlemen on the exactness of your presentations and the clarity of your thinking. I would be pleased to have you serve as jurors in any case I might present."

The boys smiled proudly.

"Let us proceed, gentlemen. May I examine the evidence? The cent?"

Josh handed Lincoln the cent. Lincoln solemnly examined each side of the coin. He peered intently at its edge turning it carefully so that he saw the entire coin.

"Will, you assert this is the coin you lost last week?" asked Lincoln.

"Yes sir."

"Tell me, if you would, sir, what is there about this particular cent that sets it off from every other cent that was minted? Will, how do you know that this is precisely the coin that you lost and absolutely not any other coin?"

"Well, um…"

"You charged your good friend, Josh, with being a thief predicated on the allegation that this coin is the exact coin that you lost, did you not?"

"I reckon I did."

"Would you care, my good sir, to retract your charge?"

Josh let out a whoop.

"I'm sorry, Josh," said Will, "I reckon you ain't a thief after all.

"Now, it's your turn, Josh," said Lincoln. "Your allegation is that your very good and honest friend Will, who just apologized to you, is a liar. Is that correct?"

"He called me a thief first and that ain't so. You proved it Mr. Lincoln."

"I did. However, whatever Will did does not excuse what you did. You still called him a liar. Will admitted that he could not prove the cent was his. Can you prove the cent is not his? Can you aver with absolute certainty that this cent could not possibly be the one that Will lost last week? And that therefore the coin is not Will's. Further, can you show that Will knew the coin was not his and yet he willfully and with full prior knowledge engaged in prevarication thus making him, in fact, a liar?"

"I don't think that I can prove that. I reckon that I ought to apologize too. Will I hadn't ought to call you liar. I'm sorry," said Josh.

"I'm proud of both of you gentleman. You were men enough to admit your misacceptations and to apologize. I hope you see how easy it is in a moment of emotional upheaval to make an accusation and how wisdom dictates that certitude is needed before such charges should be made. A man's reputation might be besmirched for no reason at all. And the most precious thing a man has is his reputation."

"Yes sir," said Will. "But, Oh, Mr. Lincoln what do we do with the cent. Might a been mine. Might rightly be Josh's."

"If its really Will's he should have it," said Josh.

"But if it's really yours you should have it," said Will.

"Gentlemen, I am happy to be able to perform a miracle that even the great and wise Solomon could not achieve." Lincoln opened his hand and showed the boys two half-cent coins.

"Thank you," said William. "I'm proud of both my brothers."

William saw that Henry was too busy talking with a pretty blond woman standing close to Dutch to notice what William just said.

"Here is mother," said Dutch. "Elise, my wife."

Dutch put his arm around the pretty blond woman with whom Henry had been conversing. Mrs. Myers smiled up at her husband and then turned to William. She was a small neat woman with twinkling blue eyes and a friendly smile. She wore a crisply starched apron over her gingham housedress.

"I am pleased to meet you," said Mrs. Myers. "We are very fond of Henry. He's been a big help to my husband and kind to the rest of my family. He has spoken about you so much that I feel like I already know you."

A small blond boy with a dirty face came running up to Henry squealing with pleasure. With great intensity he whispered something into Henry's ear and then stared pulling on him intently. Henry smiled happily and followed the boy who trotted away quickly.

"You are most kind, Ma'am," said William.

"You know I think Arch measures himself against you," said Mrs. Myers. "I gather he didn't know his father well and his father didn't seem to be the kind of man a son would want to compare himself to."

"He was a drunkard, Ma'am," said William. "No doubt he meant well and all but he was a slave to the bottle. In the end it killed him. He got into a drunken brawl at a tavern with a stranger who pulled a knife."

17

"Leaving you to act like a father at a very young age," said Mrs. Myers.

"Yes, Ma'am," said William. "I was too young to be much good at it and too proud to ask for help when I needed it. I regret being as harsh as I was, for as little reason as I had, at the time. That Arch and Henry turned out to be good men I credit to the grace of God."

"I think you deserve some credit too," said Mrs. Myers.

"Thank you, Ma'am," said William. "But I'm not so certain about that. I did what I could of what had to be done. I reckon that's as much credit as I can rightly claim."

"Maybe you should tell them and see if that's how they feel about it," said Mrs. Myers.

"Maybe I should apologize to them," said William. "I've thought on it more than once but I can't seem to find the proper time and place."

"Enough serious talking," said Dutch. "Come to dinner and meet the boarders."

William washed up and then came into the large dining room just in time to hear Mrs. Myers make an announcement.

"Nobody with a dirty face or dirty hands eats dinner in this house."

The small boy and Henry scurried out of the room.

Mrs. Myers crossed her arms over her chest.

"I said nobody."

Two of the boarders sheepishly stood up and left the room. In a short time Henry and the boy returned. The two boarders returned a few minutes later.

After all were seated Dutch made introductions. The small boy he announced with evident pride was his son, Israel. The boarders included Samuel Franklin, a small man with black hair, brown eyes, a dark complexion and a squint who worked as a desk clerk at the Illinois Hotel.

"I would of thought a hotel would provide room and board to folks that work there," said Henry.

"The hotel is in the business of selling rooms and food," said Franklin. "I work there but with what they pay me I couldn't afford to live and eat there."

"Besides the food is better here," said Mrs. Myers.

"Yes, Ma'am," said Franklin smiling.

A second boarder was a heavy set red faced man with light brown hair and dark eyes. He was dressed in a dusty black broadcloth suit. He was named Dennis Kelly. Kelly was a traveling whiskey seller who looked like he had been sampling his product rather heavily. "I offer smooth Kentucky whiskey as soft as a mother's kiss but strong as an Indiana mule. If you gentlemen would like to join me after dinner, I could demonstrate the benefits of my superior merchandise."

Henry looked tempted but he looked àt William who answered for them.

"My thanks for your kind offer," aid William. "Perhaps later on we can take advantage of it. We thought that after dinner we'd take in some of the sights of the city."

19

A third boarder was James Dorman, a tall rail thin man with a soft, but persistent cough. His hair and complexion were nearly the same shade of gray. Mr. Dorman was, in his words, a newspaperman for the Sangamo Journal. He was vague about exactly what his job duties entailed. Later, Arch guessed he sold papers on the street corner. Henry guessed he inked the presses. William guessed he was a long-term worker who did whatever odd jobs the publisher could think of.

"You've come to one of the most exciting cities in the whole state," said Dorman. "I cannot imagine a more vibrant or dynamic location for your exploration."

The fourth boarder was Leonard James, a hefty young man with brown hair and eyes who worked as a blacksmith and farm machine repairman. Despite his work he was the neatest and cleanest of the boarders. He engaged William in a discussion of the latest farm machinery and labor saving devices. They debated whether the time and cost of repairs of the sometimes-fragile machines were worth the effort saved by using the machines. Henry chimed in his opinion in support of the newest devises. William said he preferred to let others try out new machines, to discover their defects, and to fix them

before he tried the new machines.

The last boarder was Elijah Hart, a small but wiry man with sandy hair and blue eyes. He was a drayman. He owned a team of strong horses and a low wide strongly constructed wagon with reinforced axles and wheels. He hauled heavy loads and large items that could be moved no other way. He was humbly dressed in stained, but clean, work clothes. In contrast to the other talkative boarders, Hart was silent except when spoken to. Hart did not sleep at Myers but he took his meals there.

As expected, dinner was a hearty meal with fried and mashed potatoes, gravy, chicken and dumplings fried eggs, pork, beef, and pickles. For Dutch there were German sausages and sauerkraut. There was bread fresh from the oven and tomatoes from the garden. Beer, milk, lemonade and cold tea was drunk. The conversation lagged as the serious business of eating was attended to. Platters were passed and food was consumed at a steady efficient rate. When the initial appetites were dulled Mrs. Myers brought out pies, pastries and other sweets that vanished quickly.

Satisfied, the men sat back in their chairs and complimented Mrs. Myers on her cooking. Conversation picked up again on a more relaxed basis.

Kelly, the traveling whisker seller, perhaps recognizing a kindred soul turned to Henry and said, "I'll bet you can't guess the most unusual load that Mr. Hart there ever hauled in his dray."

Hart said, "That's disrespectful."

"Nonsense," said Kelly. "It's all in good fun. Go ahead and guess. If you haven't heard and you guess correctly in three tries I'll give a jug of my very finest."

Henry looked at Mrs. Myers who raised her eyebrows but did not say a word.

"I guess a marble tomb, another dray, and a steam boat," said Henry.

"In truth I've hauled all three, if you count boiler parts as a whole steam boat," said Hart. "But I don't think that's what Kelly means."

"I presume what Mr. Kelly is referring to is the time when Mr. Hart gave a ride to Mary Todd," said Mr. Myers. "Miss Todd is a member of the Todd family of Kentucky. It's one of the first

21

families of the United States. Naturally she is one of the leading lights in local Springfield society. She and her friend had traveled downtown in their latest finery one day during the rainy season by carrying shingles and putting them on the ground to form a sort of movable wooden sidewalk. It was an excellent idea. The only problem was that the streets were so full of water that after they stepped on the shingles the shingles sank completely into the mud and disappeared. The ladies successfully made it to downtown but then their supplies of shingles ran out. They were stuck without a way to get home while protecting their clothes."

"I don't know why you don't build more sidewalks in this town," said Mrs. Myers. "All the women would be thankful."

"Like I've told you, mother, I'd be happy to if someone would pay me for the work," said Dutch. "Why don't you talk to Alvan Martin, the mayor?"

"I don't trust that man," said Mrs. Myers. "Where was I? Oh yes. They wanted to protect their new clothes. In a moment of inspiration Miss Todd hailed our Mr. Hart and because of his good heart she was able to persuade him to carry her home in his dray even though he had work to do elsewhere. She created quite a stir as she rode regally home in the dray dressed in the latest fashions. She's a very pretty woman with a pleasing figure, a lively smile and bright eyes. She arrived triumphantly unsullied at home.

"Her action inspired a poem that was published in the paper and a good deal of attention both favorable and otherwise. Although we certainly do not travel in the same social circles I regard her as one of the most intelligent and well educated women I have ever met."

Mrs. Myers paused for a breath and then continued.

"Sadly, her engagement to one of our up and coming young men, Mr. Abraham Lincoln, ended unfortunately for unclear reasons. That does not bring her discredit; it only brings on unwanted gossip."

Mrs. Myers looked directly at Kelly in a challenging way. Kelly remained quiet.

Dutch invited the men out onto the broad covered porch in front of the house to smoke. Kelly said something about not mixing his pleasures and headed upstairs, presumably to drink. James remarked that he had an unfinished buggy at the smithy he had to finish that day. He left. Franklin said he'd like to stay but he had to get back to the hotel or they'd dock his pay. Dorman claimed he expected a story to "break" any minute and strode importantly off. Hart nodded politely to the assembled men and walked off.

"Well it is just us chickens left here," said Dutch. "Arch, why don't you take your brothers and Mr. Fisher to show them the city? G.W. and I can get along the rest of the afternoon without you. Be back by supper though. Supper the way Mother cooks is what you don't want to miss."

"Why don't you come with us?" asked Arch.

"Thank you, no," said Dutch. "You enjoy yourself with your brothers. I'll stay here with G.W. and make sure we still have a business going."

"Who's G.W.?" asked William.

"He's a free black man," said Arch. "His real name is George Washington Turner. Some people around here got upset when Dutch called him George Washington so we took to calling him G.W. To tell you the truth, he's a better carpenter than Dutch or me. If he wasn't black, he'd own the business and we'd work for him."

23

Arch led the men through the lobbies of the fancy hotels and the showed them fine stores of Springfield. William and Fisher were impressed by the tall buildings and the ongoing activities of the city. They walked by the government buildings they had ridden by before.

At a carriage shop, which had a raised half-sized model of a formal carriage in front, Fisher stopped to watch a group of boys who were spinning one wheel of the carriage. The afternoon sunlight sparkled on the brightly painted spokes of the wheel in a pattern of alternating dark and light.

"Stay here if you like, Mr. Fisher," said William. "We'll see you back at Myers for supper."

Fisher stared intently at the spinning wagon wheel and gave no response to William. As the other men left, Fisher stood still as if rooted into the ground and ignored them.

Chapter Four

Monday, May 31, 1841 Springfield, Illinois

In high spirits Henry and Arch led William to west fifth street across the street from Hoffman's row.

"I promised a friend of mine in Clary's Grove that I would say 'Hello' to a friend of his when I came to Springfield," explained Henry. "I hope he's in at this hour."

The men came to an office labeled "Logan & Lincoln Attorneys And Counsellors At Law." They knocked on the door. On hearing, "Come in." from a raspy voice they entered. They found a scene that verged on the humorous. Two men as different as day and night but each of remarkably ugly appearance were inside. One was sitting at a desk and the other was standing as they talked. Judge Stephen T. Logan was a slight, short man with a high forehead and gray curly hair that swept back from his face. His features were mismatched and his face was wizened and gnome-like. He sat in a chair making him appear even shorter. He was dressed in a simple but well made suit.

Towering over the older man was a man who stood at an awkward posture. He leaned forward with stooped shoulders appearing to be angular and somehow unfinished. His hands and feet seemed too big for the rest of his body but his chest was thin and his legs seemed too long for the rest of him. His face was notably homely and sad with sunken gray eyes and cheekbones that formed sharp planes. The man's hair was dark and rumpled as if he had been in a high wind. The man had a thin, nearly a scrawny neck with a prominent Adam's apple. There was an air of sadness about him.

25

"Judge Logan, Mr. Lincoln," said Arch, "I, We don't mean to intrude. If you're busy we can come back later."

"I believe we're about done," said Abraham Lincoln in a high-pitched but not unpleasant voice. "The judge was kindly instructing me in some of the finer points of the law."

"I was trying to convince my young friend, that it is an essential point of the law to set and collect reasonable fees for services well done," said Judge Logan in a raspy voice. "To do so requires that one keep correct and timely records. I suspect this is a conversation that Mr. Lincoln and I will have again."

"I'd like to introduce you to my brothers," said Arch. "William is the oldest. He's a widower who lives with his younger children on a farm he owns in Warren County. He's a deacon in the local Methodist church."

William shook hands with the judge and Lincoln.

"You may have seen Henry before," said Arch. "He lives about twenty miles from here with his wife, son and a new baby girl on a farm in Clary's Grove. I get to see him a lot more than I get to see William."

Henry shook hands with the judge and Mr. Lincoln.

"I hope you gentlemen will excuse me," said Logan. "I have guests at home I need to attend to." He gathered his papers and left the office wishing all the men a hearty good evening.

"Why don't you sit down?" asked Lincoln. "I'm guessing that you don't need legal advice."

"No sir," said Henry. "We don't need a lawyer. I'm a sort of a distant neighbor to Jack and Hannah Armstrong in Clary's Grove.

When I told them I was going to Springfield they asked me to tell you "Hello."

"How kind," said Lincoln. "They were friends to me when I had very few other friends. They kept me in food and clothing when I had no means to repay them. How are they?"

"Jack's still as strong as a bear," said Henry. "Hannah's still a pretty woman."

"Strong as a bear even though his pelt's got white streaks in it?" asked Lincoln. "That sounds like Jack. I suppose you've heard how we met."

"William hasn't," said Henry.

"When I came to New Salem where Mr. Armstrong and his friends were congregated I was a young buck fresh off the farm," said Lincoln. "There was a group of young men in the town known as the Clary's Grove Boys who were as rough as cobs. Just high spirited sorts without a touch of meanness in the whole group. I was known as something of a wrestler so Jack Armstrong, who was the toughest of the group, decided he'd have to clean my plow for me."

Lincoln collapsed into a chair and slouched into a gangly but comfortable, position resting on his spine with his knees raised.

"We opened the tussle in the grass near by Offut's store. Jack commenced to hammer me like I was an anvil. I responded by chopping at him like he was a tree. Jack threw me over his hip and rolled me along the ground head over heels. I caught him in a headlock and whacked away at his face. We staggered through every mud puddle in the street and excavated several news ones until the local hogs thought we'd joined their clan. Finally about sundown Jack decided that he had enough of bruising his fists on my face so he let up. Later on he said he quit because he was afraid he'd get

27

home too late for dinner. The rest of the boys circled around me. They seemed determined to continue the dance where Jack had left it. Then Jack pushed through them all. He declared that he was beaten fair and square. He said if the fight was to continue it would be with him and me together against the whole lot of the boys. I reckon they'd all had ruckuses with Jack before because that was the end of the fight. Jack and I have been friends ever since."

"Mr. Lincoln's one of our leading citizens," said Arch. "He started as a farmer's son and taught himself the law. Now he's a state assemblyman and a partner to a former judge. He started as a scrub, a common man like us, and now he's a man who works with his head instead of his hands."

William eyed the man in front of him skeptically. Lincoln's too short pants legs were pulled half way up his calves allowing an observer to see that his socks were mismatched. His suit was travel-strained and his hair stuck up at odd angles from when he ran his fingers through it. Even so, there was something about the man that commanded respect. An air of melancholy hung about him like a well-worn cloak. But when he smiled his gray eyes sparkled and a transformation came over his face until he seemed almost handsome.

"I know my appearance is not the most elegant," said Lincoln. "I was riding the court circuit until earlier today when I came to see the judge about a point of law I needed instruction in. Even at my best I own that I am no beauty. I remember once I met a particularly pretty young woman who fair took my breath away. In a moment of reckless weakness I told her that she was the most beautiful woman that I'd ever seen. She looked me up and down and answered that I was the ugliest man in the world. I told her that what she was not a reply that a Christian woman should make. She responded that it was the truth and asked me what she should have done. I told her that she should have done what I did when I spoke to her. She should have lied."

Lincoln wrapped his arms around his knees and rocked back and forth as he laughed. Arch and Henry doubled over with laughter. William laughed in a more restrained way.

"What's it like to be a lawyer?" asked Henry. "I've thought that I could do that."

"Well, I started by reading about the law," said Lincoln. "I really had only one year of schooling. That was at a little "blab" school. Every student read the lesson out loud together. It made quite a commotion. Now, I reckon the teacher didn't know much more than the better students. Luckily for me, I had friends who took an interest and steered me through some very good books. Later on I read everything I could put my hands on. I learned surveying and later on I learned the law that way. I don't think there's a better way to learn than by studying the basic books on your own. I used to stay up nights reading after the day's work was done until I mastered the books. If you're serious I can recommend Blackstone first. Then you could look at Greenleaf, Chitty and the two books by Story."

"Did you neglect your family to read?" asked William. The disapproval was evident on his voice.

"No," said Lincoln sadly. "I regret that I had no family. I still don't. There was a time when I thought I might... Pardon me gentlemen. I did not mean to burden you with my problems. With women I'm like the pig with a Latin book. I study and study but I just can't seem to speak the language."

"You ought to ask William about that," said Henry with an edge to his voice.

"No," said William. "I only knew only one woman well, my dearly departed Sarah. I never did figure out why she wanted me when she could have had many a better man. I only know that women are really notional. If someday a woman takes a notion that

29

she sees something in you that you don't see in yourself, you ought to give yourself a chance to see if she's right."

Lincoln nodded thoughtfully. He seemed to be about to respond when Henry jumped in.

"William doesn't approve of a man dreaming," said Henry.

"That's not fair," said Arch. "William doesn't approve of a man acting like a mooncalf while his family suffers because he fails to take care of his responsibilities."

"And you think I do that?" asked Henry narrowing his eyes and clenching his fists.

"I don't," said William.

"Neither do I," said Arch.

"Well I don't!" exclaimed Henry. Henry's face reddened and clenched fists tightened. Lincoln quickly intervened.

"If you gentlemen are really interested, I reckon there were two events that pushed me in the direction of the law. The first happened when I briefly owned a small country store. Managing that enterprise I managed to progress from abject and total poverty to a high level of indebtedness during that time. A man who was headed west with an overloaded wagon wanted me to pay him to leave behind a barrel full of unwanted effects and household plunder. I did not want it but finally he persuaded me to pay him fifty cents for what he would have discarded for nothing anyway. I obliged him then when I looked through the barrel months later I found an old but complete edition of Blackstone's Commentaries. I fair read wore the words off the pages by reading so hard while I further deepened my debts by neglecting to attend to the store. And it may be a good thing that I did.

"A little later I built a scow and commenced to actually make some actual cash money delivering travelers to steamers moving along the Ohio River. Now, John and Lin Dill had an exclusive license to ferry passengers across the river right there. They hailed me one day and persuaded me under false pretences to accompany them to the home of Squire Pate where they swore to a warrant charging me with illegally transporting passengers across the river. They swore under solemn oath that they had seen me carry a passenger to a steamer that stopped to pick them up. I was in a stew being totally unprepared and the charges being the truth. But I plucked up my courage. I asked the Squire that, even if it was true that the Dill brothers had the exclusive license to ferry people *across* the river, how did that make it illegal for me to carry people who missed the Dill ferry *to* passing steamers in midstream? The Dill brothers thought that was a minor quibble but the squire held that it was sound legal reasoning. Despite the protests of the Dill brothers, he dismissed the warrant and invited me to visit him on law days when he sat as justice of the peace and adjudicated various legal disputes. I learned a lot of practical law and saw how a man could be even handed with rich and poor alike.

"Some of my neighbors attended law days as though they were high drama and Shakespeare's tragedies. For me they awakened something in my mind and my breast and I came to make the law my life's work and satisfaction."

Henry, whose complexion had faded back to its normal color, turned toward Lincoln. "William disapproves of politics too."

"I don't like it when a man gets political fever so strong that he neglects his family and his work," said William.

"My first law partner, Major Stuart, did that," said Lincoln.

"To tell the truth, I think that politics is too loud and rowdy," said William. "For many men it's just an excuse to stop working and get drunk. I leave that to others."

"There is where your opinion and mine part company," said Lincoln. "In this country we don't have a king or an aristocracy to tell us what to do. Politics is the responsibility and the duty of all of us. I agree it can provide an excuse to get drunk or to raise a ruckus. I agree that sometimes the words get hot, rough and personal. We're a young country. Maybe we'll get better at governing ourselves as we get more practice at it. But imperfect as it is, politics is what we have to work with."

Lincoln fell into the cadence of a campaign speech. "Strong and heart-felt debate, contention and partisanship have been part of what makes the United States what it has become. It's part of our heritage. Jefferson and Hamilton exchanged hard words and offered different views of the future of our country. Their disputes helped us chose our course. Vigorous exchanges in the newspapers and broadsides, like the Federalist papers before the adoption of the constitution, helped define the questions to be argued. George Washington called out the army to fight the Whiskey rebellion to insure the authority of the federal government. Henry Clay contended with great fervor and at the same time with great respect for his opponents, even Andrew Jackson. Time and again harsh words in the house of government has helped us avoid bloodshed on the ground outside. We will not resolve the thorny differences that strain the bonds of brotherhood by polite words over tepid cups of tea. We need the rough and tumble exchange of verbal thrust and parry. Will slavery be extended to new states and territories? I argue that slavery is an evil that should not spread. However, I accept, and even defend, the existence of slavery, as evil as I believe it to be, in those states where it now flourishes. Sadly, it is the law of the land and we must obey the law, as it is, however ungodly and odious it is, until we can correct the law itself. In our system I have to defend my belief both against those who want to expand slavery and against those who wish to destroy slavery throughout the land."

Lincoln looked around him and his color rose.

"I apologize," said Lincoln. "Attorneys and politicians both tend to fall on speech making with the slightest provocation, like a sot falls on a full bottle. I am both an attorney and a politician so I lay claim to both excuses."

"I thought you were fixing to go into a real stem winder there," said Arch.

"Let's speak of more pleasant things. Mr. Trailor, this is your first time in our city. What do you think about it?"

"It seems right lively to me," said William. "I've never seen so many people in one place at one time. There are buildings going up all over the place so I reckon it's a good place for a carpentry enterprise. On the other hand, I'd not call it a pretty place."

"That reminds me of something," said Lincoln. "A man applied to Thompson Campbell, Secretary of State of Illinois, for the use of a certain government building for a series of lectures. When Campbell inquired as to the subject of the lectures the man replied with great seriousness that they were to be about the second coming of the Lord. Campbell allowed as how the man could use the building but he added that in his opinion it wouldn't be of any use. Campbell advised the man not to waste his time in this city. He said if the Lord had been in Springfield once he would not come the second time."

Again Lincoln rocked back in his chair laughing in his high-pitched voice. Henry and Arch laughed so hard that they seemed likely to fall from their chairs. William showed only a wintry smile on his face.

33

"We have imposed enough on your time," said William. "I thank you for your kind words. I'm always happy to meet friends of my brothers. I think we should go now."

After the brothers each shook hands with Lincoln they excused themselves politely and left the office.

"He's a funny man," said William. "Even if he did break off his engagement with Miss Todd. I guess you wanted me to meet a local character."

"He's much more than that," said Arch. "He pulled himself up by dint of his efforts to become one of the leading lawyers in the whole state. He's a state assemblyman. I'll wager that someday he'll be in congress."

"Maybe," said William. "However I doubt it will be in my lifetime."

"Hattie gave me a shopping list," said Henry, "I have a strict set of instructions about ribbons, fabrics, thread, colors, buttons and such like."

"You'd best get to it then," said William. "You don't want to disappoint the pretty little lady."

"I've got something to show William," said Arch. "Why don't we meet at the blacksmith's when we all finish?"

When Henry tracked down the blacksmith, Leonard James, at his forge he found that William and Arch were not yet there. Within a little more than half an hour William and Arch joined him. William asked if Fisher had been by, and James said he had not seen the man since dinner. They disputed amiably and without anger about whether or not a heavy harrow that James was constructing could be pulled by a single healthy workhorse through a muddy field. James assured the men a year old colt could pull it through deepest quicksand. William maintained that a brace of workhorses in their prime could not pull it through a field until the dew dried off. Close to suppertime all the men headed back to Myers boarding house together.

Dutch was pleased to learn that the Trailors had visited Lincoln.

"He's an honest lawyer," said Dutch. "When I first come to Springfield I speak bad English. Worse even than now I mean to say."

Dutch smiled at the memory.

"A man had me do work on his house," said Dutch, "Then he wouldn't pay me. Mr. Lincoln went to him and told him if he doesn't pay me Mr. Lincoln would get the judge to at least let me take back the lumber and nails I use. He asks the man if he would rather pay the bill or live in a house with holes in the walls and the roof. He pays the bill."

Mrs. Myers said, "It was only with difficulty that Father was able to get Mr. Lincoln to accept any payment. Mr. Lincoln insisted that since there was no trial there should be no bill. He said most of his clients wanted the fuss and feathers of a full trial before they felt he'd earned his fees.

"He said he didn't usually get paid for swapping whoppers. Lincoln said the man stretched the truth when he claimed he couldn't pay father but he himself won the debate when he outstretched him by his threats of what a judge would do. Later we learned that at that time he was mostly supporting himself by felling trees, chopping wood and splitting rails for fences.

"One thing I admire is that like my husband, Mr. Lincoln pulled himself up by his bootstraps. He was a hired hand, a store clerk, a flat boat pilot, a merchant, a surveyor and a postmaster all with somewhat limited success before he taught himself the law."

"His persistence is admirable," admitted William. "He must be quite the local hero to have so many supporters. To change the subject have you seen Mr. Fisher? We left him at a carriage makers shop and we haven't seen him since."

"He has not returned here," said Dutch.

"He was acting strangely for the last day or so," said William. "I'm concerned."

"Why don't you check the room and see if he came in and got his belongings?" asked Dutch.

Arch quickly went up the stairs and returned.

"Everything is still there."

At the supper table none of the boarders could recall seeing Fisher since dinner. Franklin said he was certain the man had not come into the hotel. Dorman said he had not seen the man anywhere. James repeated what he said earlier at his smithy that Fisher had not been by. Hart said he had a job of work outside the city and only returned in time for supper. Kelly seemed uncertain what Fisher even looked like. Although the food Mrs. Myers provided was both ample and well cooked, the absence of Fisher lent something of a pall over the meal. Only Kelly, who acted and smelled as if he had been imbibing his own whiskey samples, seemed unaffected.

After the meal, William, Henry and Arch decided to search for Fisher. William asked Dutch for a list of doctors and their addresses saying he would check that out. Henry said he'd noticed that Fisher had an eye for good horseflesh. He offered to check out livery stables and horse sellers. Arch said he knew a few people who had moved to Springfield from Warren County. He said he would see if Fisher had chanced upon old friends and had supper with them. Each of the boarders promised to keep an eye out for Fisher as they went about town that evening.

Arch returned in a few hours. Arch told Dutch that none of the people who moved from Warren County had seen Fisher but they all promised to watch for him. "I talked to a family heading back to Warren County," said Arch. "They promise to alert families they stay with along the way. I have no doubt that they will. There's no unsavory piece of gossip that these people will not pass along as gospel."

William returned shortly after Arch did. He said he talked with every doctor in town. William said there were no unidentified patients in town but that the doctors all they would notify him if an unknown patient fitting Fisher's description turned up.

Henry returned after dark. He said he had been to the livery stables and talked to the better known horse sellers but to no avail.

"Of course, everybody thinks of himself as a great horse trader. There's no way I could see everybody who owns a horse," said Henry.

Upon their return, the various boarders said they had not seen Fisher either. Later that evening Kelly told other drinkers in Keys' tavern about Fisher's disappearance. "I don't understand," said Kelly. "Why are the Trailors are so concerned about a hired hand with no family. Obviously, they know something they're not telling the rest of us."

Chapter Five

Tuesday, June 1, 1841 Springfield, Illinois

The next morning the Trailor brothers got up early before breakfast and resumed the search. They returned without Fisher once again. Over flapjacks, corndodgers, eggs and black coffee the Trailor brothers discussed the matter with the Myers and the boarders.

"I reckon I should see the sheriff," said William. "Mr. Fisher won't be happy. He hates it when other people root around in his business. He'll be like a horse with a bur under his saddle but I don't know what else to do."

"Why don't you let me talk to the sheriff?" asked Arch. "I'm a citizen of the town and he might hear me out better. He's got an election coming up and even if he has no opponent so far he's not a well respected man so he's likely to be more accommodating than he usually is right now."

"I did some roostering around in this town when I was single," said Henry. "I can talk to some folks I knew back then who aren't what you'd call upstanding citizens. They might have heard something, if something shady happened."

"Maybe I can backtrack Mr. Fisher's trail," said William. "There might be some sign that I missed yesterday."

The Trailor brothers headed out energetically once more.

Arch presented himself at the sheriff's office. Jim Maxey a large, slab sided man with ebony brown eyes, sandy hair, and a world-weary expression on his tanned deeply lined face, was making coffee. He was a man in the prime of his life.

"I'd like to see Caleb Young," said Arch.

"So would I," said Maxey. "If the sheriff was here I could go home and get some sleep. It was a rough night last night in two of the taverns so I didn't get much shuteye. Unluckily for both of us Sheriff Young is out of town right now. You're stuck because you'll have to tell me. I'm stuck because the other deputy, Alonzo Wickersham, is somewhere drinking better coffee than I'm making."

Arch explained that Fisher was missing all night without explanation. He told the deputy what the Trailor brothers had done and asked if Maxey could help.

"You didn't think to ask the undertaker if he had any unexplained bodies?" asked Maxey.

"No," said Arch with a startled look on his face. "I didn't think of that at all."

"Don't worry," said Maxey. "I'd know if there were any extra dead bodies in Springfield. We got nobody in jail except the usual lot of drunkards, brawlers and felons."

"Can you suggest anything else we could do?" asked Arch.

"No," said Maxey. "You've done all that you could including telling me. You don't know for certain that there's anything wrong. Even if he left his things in Springfield, he might just have decided to leave town. Maybe he went back to the farm or maybe he headed off West. There's many that do without so much as a fare-thee-well. I'll keep a look out for him. I'll tell the sheriff when he gets back."

The coffeepot boiled.

"Would you like some coffee?" asked Maxey. He took a rag in his hand and lifted the coffeepot off the Franklin stove. Maxey found a battered cup and poured the oily black coffee into it.

"Thank you but I'd best be going back," said Arch looking uneasily at the coffee.

"You board with the Myers, right?" asked Maxey.

"Yes," answered Arch.

"No wonder you don't want some of this," said Maxey.

Arch turned to go.

"Is Fisher a rich man?" asked Maxey.

"I'm not sure," said Arch. "When we were children we used to say that he was so tight that he must have quite a haul put away, in gold doubloons, no less, but William always said that talk made as much sense as the wind did when it blew through the leaves of a tree. He said Fisher had no land, no crops, no house, and no animals except for an old rawboned horse. He said Fisher only worked small jobs mostly for room and board. He reckoned Fisher had to be tight to live and the only gold Fisher saw was moonbeams. Why do you ask?"

"Well, it seems to me that rich men collect trouble like dogs collect fleas," said Maxey. "Poor men have to work a little harder at it."

Arch left the sheriff's office and stood on the wooden sidewalk wondering where to go next. He decided to walk along the streets and stop where a visitor might stop. He talked to people each time he stopped but nobody admitted seeing a man like Fisher. Toward mid day he began to feel hungry so he went back to Myers.

William was there already complaining that Fisher was harder to track than smoke on a foggy day. He reported that he had no success at all. A few minutes later Henry came in smelling of tobacco smoke and cheap whiskey. He said he'd talked to a few of the men he used to run with but he had learned nothing of use. William noticed Henry's condition but only told him he should clean up before dinner or Mrs. Myers might not let him eat at the table.

At dinner William announced that he would be leaving to return to his farm and family.

"There's nothing more we can do here," said William. "I've been away longer than I planned already."

"How's Fisher going to get home when he turns up?" asked Mrs. Myers calmly.

"Hey, you can't leave yet," said Kelly suddenly indignant. "You haven't even taken me up on sampling my whiskey."

"If he turns up here Arch can send him to Henry and I'll figure a way to get him back," said William.

"Maybe Dutch can keep his traveling kit," said Henry. "Would that be all right?"

"Done," said Dutch. "When he returns we'll send him on his way home."

"There's a news story here somewhere," insisted Dorman. "I can fair smell it. Return of the prodigal or stolen by Gypsies. Maybe even a special edition story."

"There's probably something unwholesome behind all this," said Franklin. "Something unchristian."

"I hope the poor man is safe and sound wherever he is," said Mrs. Myers.

Hart looked on intently but he did not say anything.

William retrieved the dearborn and his horse from the livery stable. William and Henry said polite good-byes to Dutch and Mrs. Myers before heading out of town.

Dutch turned to Arch and said, "Back to work. There's plenty for you to do young man."

William and Arch headed northwest out of town by one road at first. Then, they returned and then headed northwest on a different road toward Clary's Grove and Warren County.

Chapter Six

Friday, June 4, 1841 Springfield, Illinois

Three days later, Henry returned to resume the search. He and Arch enlisted help from two of Henry's friends from Clary's Grove who had traveled with him. A few people from Warren County who knew Mr. Fisher earlier, but who now resided in Springfield, assisted. They were people who Arch had spoken to earlier about Mr. Fisher. The boarders at the Myers also helped. They searched through Springfield one more time. Kelly dragged Henry through all the taverns and shops that sold whiskey, asking in each if a man of Fisher's description had been seen. Kelly insisting on having a drink in each place. If he had not sold the place whiskey, he complained loudly about the poor quality of the whiskey they served. Henry broke up three fights Kelly started and then fled from him. Bruised, bloody, drunk and dirty Henry returned to Myers and fell into bed. Dissatisfied with the result of his tavern expedition, Kelly went off to seek another kindred soul and find another tavern to drink in.

Samuel Franklin talked to as many ministers as he could locate during the entire day asking if Fisher had come to them for assistance, or if assistance had been sought by another for someone who fit Fisher's appearance. All of them pled ignorance. He returned with a bladder full of tea and coffee and his ears full of pieties.

James Dorman talked to reporters he knew from every newspaper in town. He collected a series of touching stories about missing husbands, and sons. He was regaled with tales of lost children reclaimed in miraculous ways. But he learned nothing about Fisher. He pondered the possibility of an article about unexplained

43

disappearances but he gave it up as too boring. Full of whiskey and complaints about deadlines and unforgiving editors he reeled back on unsteady legs.

Leonard James and Elijah Hart looked through the back alleys

and dead end streets in the poorer sections of Springfield searching for clues. More than one group of rowdies looked them over and wisely decided that there was easier prey elsewhere. The two men came away with a greater understanding of the mean streets of Springfield. They also had a satisfying discussion of the promise of new machinery under development. Unfortunately, they came up empty on obtaining new information about Fisher.

Henry's friends from Clary's Grove and the former Warren County residents retraced Mr. Fisher's step in hopes that fresh eyes would see what others had missed.

The men sober enough to converse at the end of the day compared notes and agreed that everything they could do had been done. At Dorman's suggestion Henry wrote up an advertisement asking that if anyone knew about the location of a man of about fifty years of age, with three scars over his right eye, wearing homespun clothing, who disappeared while visiting Springfield on May 31st. Dorman took it to the Sangamo Journal and promised it would come out in the next edition.

Dorman also promised to take the ad to the rival paper, the Illinois State Register. "Although it probably won't help," Dorman said, "people are so used to reading only lies and exaggerations in that bad waste of good paper that they won't think Mr. Fisher's missing at all."

Phineus Andrew and Jason English, formerly of Warren County, talked about the search as they walked to their homes.

"The Trailors are putting considerable time and effort into searching for that bad tempered old coot, Mr. Fisher," said Andrews.

"Well, he came to town with them," said English. "They're responsible men and they're worried about him."

"My wife heard that Mr. Fisher is supposed to be a rich man," said Andrews.

"Like that horse you tried to sell me was supposed to be healthy?" asked English.

"Forget the horse," said Andrews. "You didn't buy him anyway."

"I couldn't buy him," answered English. "By the time I came to look at him the second time he was dead."

"My wife, wonders who the money went to," said Andrews "She says if it went to the Trailors, well, maybe they hurried their inheritance along. She thinks they might have killed him."

"I Thank God she's married to you and she's not married to me," said English.

Arch found Mr. Lincoln headed toward the livery stable. Lincoln expressed his regret that he could be of little assistance. Lincoln reminded Arch that he had never seem Fisher and after extracting a description Lincoln promised that he would look for Fisher as he traveled the court circuit and also when he returned to Springfield after the circuit concluded.

"It won't be long this time. Two weeks or so and I'll be back here. How much can happen in two weeks anyway?"

"Can I ask you a question?" asked Arch.

45

"It appears that you have already," answered Lincoln. "So lay on, McDuff."

"You know G.W. He works as hard as a White man, constructs as well and talks as well but he was a slave. Somebody used to own him. Some say that God ordained that there would be master and slave. Others say just as loud that God insists that we free the slaves. I don't know how that could be both ways. They say that George Washington owned slaves and so did Thomas Jefferson. But it don't seem right."

"George Washington freed his slaves in his will. Thomas Jefferson said, 'When I think of slavery and remember that God is just I tremble for the future of my country.'"

"I wish I had your words, Mr. Lincoln when somebody gets to talking about slavery I can't think of what I might say."

"You might try this, Mr. Trailor. Ask him to prove conclusively the right to enslave. If A can enslave B, why can not B snatch up the same argument and prove equally that B should enslave A? You say that A is white and B is black. It is *color* then? The lighter has the right to enslave the darker? Take care. By this rule, you are to be the slave of the first man you meet with a fairer skin than your own. You say that it is not color exactly. You say that whites are *intellectually* the superiors of blacks and therefore have the right to enslave them? Take care again. By this rule, you are to be the slave of the first man you meet with an intellect superior to your own. You say you have a *legal claim* to enslave another? Very well. Another can make a *legal claim* to enslave you."

Chapter Seven

Friday June 4, 1841 Warren County, Illinois

William Trailor drove the tired horse into the barn at his farm and climbed down stiffly. He felt all of his years acutely. He unhitched the horse. Then he rubbed down the horse, saw to it that it had food and water. He hung the harness in its accustomed place. William inspected the dearborn thinking that he needed to remember to grease the axles before he used it again. William picked up his kit and headed toward the house.

The house was a rambling two-story building. The original floor plan was evident to an observer even though a series of somewhat haphazard additions had been added at both ends of the original structure. It was functional rather than esthetic but somehow the whole house achieved an unexpected level of harmony.

Cassandra Trailor met him at the door. Cassandra was a tall, strikingly pretty twenty-year-old woman with hair the color of copper, robin's egg blue eyes and a freckled face. She wore a simple housedress with an apron over it.

"Welcome home, father," she said. "The boys should be along to eat dinner soon."

William looked at his daughter with unusual intensity. Cassandra thought he looked pale and drawn. In the mid-day light he had the appearance of a tired old man. Somehow he seemed to lack the energy and vitality, which usually gave him the aura of a man half his age. Cassandra was used to William challenging his sons to contests of strength and endurance on the farm. She found the change frightening and disturbing.

"Why do you look at me like that?" she asked.

"I was just thinking how much you resemble your mother," said William. "Sarah was a beautiful woman, you know. And you have that same beauty. I was thinking that you shouldn't be wasting yourself taking care of your old father and your brothers."

"I certainly don't think I'm wasting myself here," said Cassandra. Her eyes flashed.

"Yes," said William. "You have your mother's temper too. Martha and Ruth are married, and happy as far as I can tell. Thomas, Gideon, and Matthew are on their own and doing as well as any man can hope to. My brother Arch is a partner in a carpentry business and even brother Henry finally seems to be well established. You're still here looking after me and the younger boys. Maybe I've taken advantage of that. It's comfortable having you here. I'd be sorry to see you leave. I'd miss you. But maybe I've been keeping you at my home when you should be making your own home."

"Father I love it here," said Cassandra. "I'm not wasting away like some old maid. I haven't complained."

"Well, yes, but you might not complain. You might think it's your responsibility. You might not even mind it too much now. Maybe later on you'd regret not following up on your chances. I'd like to see you happily wed, you know. Your mother and I were, on the whole, well pleased to be together. I'd like to see you have a husband and children before I'm dead."

"You'll be alive for a long time yet," said Cassandra with tears in her eyes. "I don't know why you're talking like this. You never have before."

"Maybe I should have," said William. "I've been thinking about it for some time."

William turned to look out of the window at the green fields into which he had put so much of his life.

"This was a difficult trip, Cassie. Things happened that made me think about difficult things in my life like how I was too strict with my brothers growing up, and how I might be holding you here for my convenience."

When he turned back he saw that tears were trickling down Cassandra's face. William touched her face and then awkwardly gave her a hug.

"I didn't want to make you cry, Cassie," he said.

"I love you, Papa."

"I love you too, Cassie."

"I'd better get ready for dinner," said Cassandra drying her eyes on her apron. "The boys will be in soon."

She headed for the kitchen. William turned to the window again and stood looking out. In his mind's eye he saw the farm as it used to be when he and Sarah were younger. The hard work they did seemed easier in retrospect. Sometimes they were so happy that they did not even recognize that the hard times they had were hard.

With a pang of familiar sadness he remembered the babies buried in the graveyard. The sweet smell of wild flowers mixed with the earth smell as he dug tiny graves. All too soon the small coffins were lowered into the ground. Sarah stayed outside in the graveyard well into the night mourning her twins, David and Jonathan. Somehow the tragedy brought them even closer together. When all the other children were born healthy and survived the inevitable childhood diseases they felt God had blessed them. William saw Sarah as a beautiful young bride. He watched as hard work and care marked her face and her body. However, she always remained beautiful to him, even when the wasting disease carried her away. She rested now near her beloved twins. She was waiting for him to be beside her. Waiting more patiently than she had when she was alive William thought. He had an almost invisible smile on his face.

Distantly he heard the sounds of his sons coming in from the field and cleaning up at the pump before coming in for dinner. William allowed himself an unusual additional moment of melancholy contemplation before he turned back into the room.

Daniel and Enoch came into the dinning room with the energy and presence of a force of nature. They were sturdy, strong young men with blond hair blue eyes and weathered complexions. Although Enoch was taller and heavier than his brother was, sometimes people who did not know them well confused one brother with the other. Daniel was quicker to smile and laugh than his brother was. Enoch was more serious and once his mind had been made up he was almost impossible to turn in another direction. Together they worked as a team. Confronted with a task what one could not figure out how to do, the other would figure it out.

"Welcome home, father," said Daniel.

"I'm glad you're back," said Enoch.

Uncharacteristically, William gave each man a quick hug.

"I'm happy to be back with you all," said William.

They went into the dining room and sat at the long table. Cassandra brought out platters of fried chicken, fried eggs, corn bread, fried potatoes, and boats of gravy and a jar of strawberry preserves. There were fresh vegetables from the garden including sweet corn on the cob, and snap beans. There were pitchers of fresh milk and a pot of hot coffee. Daniel and Enoch bent into the food with gusto and seriousness. William and Cassandra ate more slowly pacing themselves.

"Of all the food I ate on my trip," said William; "I didn't find any that matched yours, Cassie."

"It's good," said Enoch. Daniel nodded enthusiastically.

"Thank you, kind sirs," said Cassandra brightly.

Almost by themselves Daniel and Enoch emptied most of the platters. Cassandra picked up the empty platters and carried them to the kitchen. She returned with rhubarb and cherry pies, which were quickly cut and consumed. At last Daniel and Enoch seemed sated. They pushed their chairs back from the table and started the conversation.

"I want you to take a look at Betsy," said Daniel. "She seems to be off her food and her milk production is down."

"That new rooster is the General Washington of chickens," said Enoch. "You might think about getting some more hens."

"I'd like to put some more vegetables into the garden," said Cassandra. "I can show you where I'd like to have the ground plowed."

William pushed his chair back.

"It's good to be home," said William. "I missed you. I know that you can run this farm as well as I can. Part way to Springfield I thought to myself that I shouldn't stay too long or you'd all figure out that you can run this place as well as I can. Now I think you knew it all along."

"I want to hear about the cow, the rooster, the garden and anything else that came up while I was away," said William. "But before that we need to talk about what happened on the trip. I notice that you didn't ask about Mr. Fisher. Does that mean that the rumors have reached here already?"

Cassandra looked at Daniel and Enoch. Daniel raised his eyebrows.

"We know that you would do nothing to hurt another person but even before you got home we heard rumors that you had done away with Fisher to steal his money," said Daniel.

"Mr. Fisher disappeared in Springfield," said William. "Arch, Henry, Mr. Fisher and I went out to see the sights. Mr. Fisher got interested in a carriage building shop and we went off to see a lawyer, Mr. Lincoln said that Arch knew and Henry's neighbor knew. He was quite a character although they were more taken with him than I was. Anyway, Mr. Fisher didn't come to the boarding house for supper. Then he didn't come to the boarding house at all. We searched for him and we got other people to look for him too. We never found him. That's the whole thing.

"On the way home, I stayed with of the same people we stayed with on the way there. I guess they found the story strange. Well, it is strange. I noticed that they treated me differently. They talked like they didn't believe me. They looked at me suspiciously and acted like they didn't want their children to be around me. I swear in one house the husband stayed awake all night with a rifle close to hand."

"That doesn't make sense," said Enoch. "If you'd been a sneak you would have kept the story to yourself."

"Before long, I found the story had gone before me like a prairie fire pushed by the winds. People started asking me what had happened before I had a chance to tell it myself. Mr. Fisher kept getting richer and richer in the stories until he could have bought the whole county."

"You know there have always been stories that he had a pile of gold somewhere" said   It used to be pirate gold. Then it was a hidden gold mine. I don't know what kind of gold it is now," said Daniel.

"I've never been treated like a pariah before," said William. "I can't say that I care for the experience."

"How can people treat you like that?" asked Cassandra. Her cheeks flushed red and her forehead furrowed. "They have no reason to even think you'd do something like that."

"Some people enjoy seeing others in the mud," said Enoch darkly. "The farther someone climbs from their roots the more some folks rejoice when they to fall. You've poured your toil and your sweat into this farm. You've made it the best in the county. You've been able to help your brothers and us children when we needed it because of your hard work every day. Others with equal opportunities have taken an easier road and now they have less. Some are envious."

"Other people are jealous that you're a deacon in the church," said Daniel. "Some people take pleasure when a church-going man has problems. It makes them feel less guilty for what they've not done."

"I feel like I'm being attacked by gnats too small to swat," said William. "It doesn't seem like there's anything I can do to protect myself."

"When Mr. Fisher turns up it'll all be over," said Cassandra.

"I'm concerned that he won't turn up," said William. "What if he took off for somewhere far away with no intention of returning?

53

What if he's really dead? May almighty God have mercy on his soul. I'm not sure that we'll ever see him again and I'm not willing to live like I've done something I should feel guilty for."

"In some strange ways," said William, "this is sort of a good thing. It reminds me that my time of earth is limited. Whatever has happened, it could have been me, instead of Mr. Fisher. I need to be sure, as best I can, that when I am gone my family is taken care of. I'm going to offer Mr. Digby the hard cash that he wants for his farm. That farm and this one together should be able to support three of you and your families, when you have families."

Cassandra looked at Daniel and Enoch.

"Thank you," said Cassandra. "You don't need to do that for us, of course, but we're grateful. Do you really think, father, this is a good time to be showing that you have gold and silver coin?"

"Much as I don't like to agree with my little sister," said Daniel, smiling, "I think that might just feed the flames. We're in no hurry. Why don't we wait?"

Cassandra stuck her tongue out at Daniel.

"Enoch said, "Much as I don't like to agree with either my sister or my brother," this time I have to concur. In time, with no more fuel, the rumor will burn itself out. Then some cow will have a calf with two heads, some farmer's daughter will run off with a traveling tinker, or somebody will get drunk and fall in a pond and eventually the whole thing will be forgotten."

William looked at his children fondly. "I'm proud of you all. I'm certain you're right. But I'm not certain I'll do what you suggest. I've been meaning to buy the Digby farm for some time. I've told him before that I could come up with the hard cash. I don't know that I'm ready to walk around with my head down like a turkey at a turkey shoot. I haven't done anything wrong and I have half a mind to really give these people something to talk about."

"Papa, promise me that you'll sleep on the idea before you act on it," said Cassandra softly.

"Very well." said William. "I promise."

William looked down the long dinning table at the places where his young children used to sit. "I remember when the table was full. The three of you, as the youngest, had to sit at the very far end and wait to see what your brothers and sisters left for you to eat. I think I'll take a nap now. The trip took a lot out of me."

He left the dining room and went upstairs.

Cassandra, Daniel and Enoch sat in silence watching their father stiffly climb the stairs.

"He looks older," said Daniel. "Despite his age, I've never thought of him as an older man."

"The trip changed him," said Enoch.

"I'm worried that he will buy the Digby farm with silver and gold just to spite the people who are gossiping about him," said Cassandra.

"He wouldn't do that would he?" asked Daniel. "That could be down right dangerous."

"He might," said Enoch. "Father is a man who's slow to anger but once angered he's awful hard to get him to change his mind."

"Like you," said Daniel.

"Where do you think I get it from?" asked Enoch.

Later that day William rode up to the Digby farm. He noted automatically that the slope of the ground insured good drainage. He knew there was a reliable spring on the property and that the buildings were kept in good repair. The farm was close to the edge of his own. Work crews could easily move from one to the other with a minimum of wasted time.

George Digby was behind his small neat house chopping wood. He was a stout man with a round red face, gray hair and small brown eyes.

"Good afternoon," said William.

"Afternoon," said Digby. "Get down from your horse and make yourself at home."

"Thanks," said William. "Don't mind if I do."

William dismounted and tied his horse to a stump.

"If you've got another ax I'll pitch in," said William.

"There's one by the wood pile but you'll have to sharpen it first," said Digby. Digby returned to chopping while William used the whetstone.

"I heard about your trip," said Digby. "What do you reckon happened to Mr. Fisher?"

"I truly wish I knew," said William. "It was like God reached down and carried him up to heaven."

"Do you think he climbed up Jacob's ladder with an angel on either arm?" Asked Digby. "Are you so sure that was the direction he traveled in? It seems to me he could have been going the other way."

56

"Do you think he was an evil man?" asked William curiously.

"Not exactly evil," said Digby. "He certainly wasn't filled with Christian kindness. He was as prickly as a bur. If something somebody said didn't sit quite right with him he'd puff up like a rooster at dawn and sputter at him or her. He walked out on Daniel Albright in the middle of the harvest because he thought one of the hired hands called him a name."

"He wasn't friendly," agreed William. "He was a hard man to get along with."

"The rumor is that you killed him for his money," said Digby.

"What do you think?" asked William.

Digby swung his ax and split the cordwood neatly.

"I think you'd better not get too close to me with that ax," said Digby. "In fact, I think you'd better leave the edge dull."

William put a piece of wood on its end on a stump. He swung the ax sharply and cleaved the wood cleanly in half. "Is that dull enough?" he asked.

"That'll do," said Digby. "In truth I don't think you killed him for his money. My idea is that you killed him because he snored."

"It was on account of his table manners," said William, "he had terrible table manners."

"How'd you get rid of the body?" asked Digby. "I bet you fed him to the horses."

"No," said William. "What I did was I put him under my arm and I snuck him up to the bar in a local tavern. I propped him up leaning against the bar and I left him there. Nobody has noticed yet."

"The truth is revealed at last," said Digby. "You're probably safe until somebody buys a round for the house. Then they would notice that he was not imbibing. And it could be a very long time before anybody buys a round for the house. You think he's dead then."

"He left his traveling kit in Springfield," said William. "He left a change of clothes here. Does that sound like Mr. Fisher?"

"No," said Digby. "He was too niggardly to leave anything behind. The man could hold a dollar so tight the eagle on it would scream."

"That's true," said William. "Speaking of eagles are you still interested in selling this place?"

"For eagles I am," answered Digby. "I'm old enough that I'd be willing to sit back and rest for a few years. I'd take a lot less for this place in hard money than I want in state bank notes. I've lost too much from having money in banks that went bust."

"I can do that," said William. "I have stored up some hard cash over the years. I reckon if this farm is combined with mine it'd be enough to support the younger children and their families."

The men worked in silence for a few minutes while Digby thought over William's offer.

"I'll sell it to you if you want," said Digby. "Have you considered how it will look to those who already think you did away with Mr. Fisher if you pay me in coin?"

"I'll not hang my head and act like I've done something wrong when I have not," said William. "People can think what they like and to blazes with them."

"All right," said Digby. "It's your neck in the noose. Just don't expect a better price because you've been chopping wood for a farm you're shortly to own."

Saturday June 5, 1841 on the road to Danville, Illinois

Abraham Lincoln with his pant legs rolled up to his thighs and standing in the middle of a stream gingerly took another step toward the far bank of the stream. Lincoln's rude carriage and swayback horse waited on the near bank. A group of men in carriages or on horse back called out encouragement and joking remarks. Judge David Davis a neatly dressed man of middle years with bright brown eyes and graying auburn hair who weighed over 200 lbs. sat in a sturdy two-horse shay.

"Well, counselor, what's taking so long?" called Davis. "The Israelites could have crossed the Red Sea three times in the time it has taken you to get half way across this creek."

"The Israelites did not have to worry about the bottom supporting the weight of the law that Mr. Lincoln has to take into account, your honor," said Leonard Swett an attorney originally from Maine who was part of the traveling party. Swett was short and red-face with blond hair, blue eyes and a muscular build.

"I thought you lobster eaters from Maine were supposed to be laconic," said Davis.

59

"We are," said Swett.

"Let's have brevity from you, Mr. Swett, and not too much of it either," said Lincoln.

"Upon reconsidering the facts of the matter in a judicial manner, not to mention a judicious manner I find for Mr. Lincoln," said Davis. "Take your time, sir. I have decided that if I am to be overturned I would rather have it happen in an appeal than in that muddy creek."

"Many and varied are the demands upon a successful lawyer in the prairie," said Lincoln. "Here I am setting the trail through a legal quagmire and you esteemed gentlemen show me such little respect. I suppose, though, I should not be surprised. My clients do not show me undue deference either. I remember when a justice of the peace who had been issuing marriage licenses for years without the authority to do so was finally challenged. He came to me for a legal opinion, I examined the facts and, of course, I had to tell him that. 'No Uncle Billy, I said, you have no right to issue marriage licenses. ' Billy became enraged and replied, 'Abe, I thought you were a lawyer, but now I know you are not. I have been doing it right along.'"

Chapter Eight

Sunday June 6, 1841 Warren County, Illinois

Increase Weaver wiped his perspiring face with his white linen handkerchief and stared down as his congregation. His sermon was not going as he imagined. His flock was attentive, in fact, you could have heard a pin drop in the silence from his first "Thou shall not kill." He was just not at all certain they were supporting what he was preaching. William Trailor sat in his usual pew as bold as brass. His younger children sat with him. His older children and their families filled nearly a quarter of the church. Not one of them seemed a bit abashed. Not one of them seemed embarrassed. William sat comfortably, nodding at times in response to what the preacher was saying. William's face was untroubled, even peaceful.

At first Weaver's practiced thunder rolled from the pulpit over the congregation like a wave breaking on a rocky shore. He was prepared for William to rise from his pew in remorse and flee from the church or to kneel and beg Weaver for forgiveness. He had practiced the sorrowful tones he would use to urge William (and other murderers in ear shot too, of course) to confess before God, and the sheriff, so he could save his soul before he was duly hung. William, however, did not seem inclined to cooperate. William sat there as placidly as if he were innocent.

Silently he cursed Mildred Goodwin for putting him in this situation. The widow Goodwin had seemed so certain of William's sinful murder. Then he reproached himself for the curse and prayed for forgiveness. He also prayed for William to do something, anything more than sit there and act like an innocent child of God.

61

Mildred Goodwin sat immediately behind the Trailor family and watched William like a hawk. Righteous indignation flared again in her breast as she thought back to her conversation with preacher Weaver. She'd had to badger and push him to prod him along like a balky mule before he had agreed to preach about the murder. After a strong start, the preacher had started to waver while William sat silently and respectfully.

Increase Weaver cleared his throat and tried to remember what he had meant to say next. His voice continued to produce solemn words automatically.

William Trailor had a heart of stone, Mildred decided. She wasn't surprised. Like father like daughter. Look at the way his harlot of a daughter treated her own dear son. Butter wouldn't melt in her mouth. She'd been polite enough, on the surface, Mildred conceded reluctantly. It was clear that underneath Cassandra was laughing at Ephraim and making fun of him. The only reasonable conclusion Mildred could draw from that, was that Cassandra had a secret attachment. She'd hunted around for the man, wondering why Cassandra would not acknowledge him. Despite having no lack of candidates, Mildred had not been able to settle on any one them. Of course, that only meant that Cassandra was sly at hiding her relationship. Sometimes Mildred thought that Cassandra was so good in her dissembling that it was likely she'd done it before with other men. She shuddered at the thought that Cassandra had nearly snared her own dear Ephraim with her worldly wiles. Mildred silently thanked the merciful Lord that she, that is, that her precious son had been spared a life married to a scarlet woman.

Increase Weaver changed the pace and pitch on his voice and headed into the home stretch of his sermon. He pulled his thoughts together to reach toward a conclusion to the sermon that made at least some sense.

The apple doesn't fall far from the tree Mildred thought. She thanked God that the momentary feeling of interest she felt for William, after he became a widower of course, had passed. He had treated her coldly, ignoring the interest she had in him as if he were not even aware of it. With a pang of regret she thought about the prosperous, well run Trailor farm. It was so hard, at times, to scratch out a living from the pitiful few acres her dearly departed Seth left her. God have mercy on his soul. She reminded herself that the Lord would not give her any task she could not complete.

William was standing. Had he succumbed at last to the twinges of what conscience he had left? Mildred's heart beat like a war drum. No. He was singing. The whole congregation was singing. The sermon was over and the final hymn was being sung. Mercy levered herself up from her pew and started to sing too. She hoped nobody noticed that she'd been gathering wool during the last part of the sermon. William must be an fiend incarnate. Even in God's house he had hardened his heart and denied the call for forgiveness. Mildred pondered what she should do next.

As the people filed out of church some edged away from William striving to avoid contact with him. Other people moved toward William. They sought him out to shake hands and speak briefly with him. Mildred Goodwin peered sharply at the members of the congregation who dared to approach him. She was troubled that so many who she had thought of as good Christians made the effort to publicly talk with William. From their smiles and friendliness, it was obvious that they did not seek him out to rebuke him.

Sensing she could do no more at the moment Mildred stalked off pointedly ignoring the Trailors. She was especially displeased that no one seemed to notice.

Eventually the Trailor family headed toward the door of the church where Increase Weaver waited nervously to speak with them.

William, Cassandra, Daniel and Enoch lagged behind the rest. Most of the family members made polite small talk to the sweating minister. When Daniel go to the door he said, "When I was listening to your sermon, I'm afraid I got lost toward the end. I didn't know what you were talking about."

"Yes," said Enoch. "You said something about lending mercy to the sorely affected. What does that mean?"

"Sometimes when I preach, I get carried away. I don't even know what I'm saying. I'm afraid that happened today."

Cassandra smiled at the minister brightly. "Sometime I'd like to hear you preach about not bearing false witness. I've always thought that included idle rumor and speculation. What do you think?"

"I've become certain that it does," said Increase Weaver miserably.

William came up to the minister last.

"I'm sorry, Mr. Trailor," said Increase Weaver. "I didn't mean to embarrass you. Well, God's truth is I did mean to. I don't know now why I thought I should. Other people kept nagging at me but I was the one who preached. Please forgive me. After that sermon the rumors will really fly."

"The will of the Lord will prevail," said William placidly. "I'm an innocent man so He will protect me in the end. I have nothing to fear. Nothing at all."

Chapter Nine

Monday June 7, 1841 Warren County, Illinois

Mildred Goodwin squared her shoulders resolutely and marched like a soldier into Alexander Baldwin's tavern. Although she had sworn never in her lifetime to pass through the door of this particular den of iniquity, she knew that her reasons were righteous and God would forgive her.

Alexander Baldwin was standing behind the bar of his establishment. He was a tall, heavyset man with a short grizzled beard and a totally bald head. His gray eyes sparkled with intelligence and wit.

"Widow Goodwin, welcome" said Baldwin. "I haven't seen you in here since poor Seth died. I seem to recall that you vowed never to pass through the door of my establishment again. I also recall how you used to come in here when Seth was enjoying himself in our humble company and drag him off home by his heels."

Mildred remembered all to clearly. "I never dragged him by his heels," she snapped.

"You're right," admitted Baldwin. "It wasn't by his heels after all. Although I do remember a time or two it was by his hair."

"That's nothing you'd have to worry about," said Mildred.

Baldwin laughed heartily and the men in the room joined in. Mildred realized that they were laughing at her expense. She nearly whirled on her heels to leave but she clung fast to her purpose and contented herself with jutting out her jaw and glaring at Baldwin.

65

"Would you care for a whiskey?" asked Baldwin.

The men in the tavern laughed again. Mildred felt her face grow warm.

"I would never spend money on the devil's brew," answered Mildred.

"Oh, its on the house," said Baldwin pouring a shot of whiskey.

Again the men laughed.

"I do not indulge," answered Mildred.

"Very well," said Baldwin. "Since you decline. Waste not want not." He downed the whiskey himself.

Mildred wished she had thought quickly enough to empty the glass onto the floor.

"Are you looking for a replacement for Seth then?" asked Baldwin. "I can recommend the character of Rafe over there by the wall. Mark's a handsome devil if that's what you want. Walter owns half a horse."

The men in the tavern howled with laughter.

Mildred felt the blood rush to her face. She knew she must be as red as a beet. It was only by dint of great effort that she held her ground. Lord; give me strength, she prayed. It is Your work that I do.

"Well, you don't want a drink. You're not looking for a new husband. And I doubt you've come here to relive old memories. Not that it hasn't been fun to renew old acquaintances; what do you want?" asked Baldwin

"I want your help," answered Mildred.

The tavern fell quiet. "Please," she said.

Baldwin picked up a rag that might have been white once. He started to wipe a glass. He held the glass up and peered at the smudged surface before he answered.

"Now in what way might I be of service to you?" asked Baldwin.

"You are the postmaster of the county," said Mildred. "I'd like you to send a letter."

"That's not a problem," said Baldwin. "You write it up and I'll send it for you."

"No," said Mildred, "I'd like you to write and send a letter in your office as postmaster of Warren County."

"What sort of letter do you want me to send?" asked Baldwin in a puzzled voice. "To who and why?"

"I'd like you, as postmaster, to send a letter about William Trailor to Springfield," said Mildred. "I want you to ask them to investigate the murder of Mr. Fisher."

She felt a charge in the air as the men in the tavern muttered about what she said. Mildred hurried on. "They wouldn't listen to the words of a poor widow woman like me. But if they heard form an important man like you they'd take it seriously."

Baldwin tried to figure out why Mildred was so interested in the matter. He did not ask her because he did not expect to believe her answer.

"It seems to me you should be talking with the sheriff," said Baldwin.

"I tried that," said Mildred. "He told me there was no evidence that a crime had been committed in Warren County. He said I should apply to where the crime was done."

In fact the sheriff had escorted her out of his office with little ceremony and less patience. He had questioned her motives severely. He had advised her that there was no evidence a crime had been committed anywhere. It was only after her repeated entreaties that he grudgingly told her she might ask the sheriff of Springfield to make inquiries. It was at that point that Mildred had decided she would need to enlist some assistance to avoid a similar reaction from the sheriff of Springfield.

Baldwin hesitated.

"Mr. Trailor was criticized in a sermon by his own pastor in his own church," said Mildred. "He sat there bold as brass and his cold heart couldn't be melted even by his own minister."

"Yeah," said Baldwin. "I think I heard something about that."

"You know Mr. Fisher was rich," said Mildred. "William Trailor bought the Digby farm for gold coin."

"I definitely heard about that too," said Baldwin.

"Piety Adams told me that she heard from Prudence Johnson that William Trailor was overheard by someone boasting that Mr. Fisher died and willed him money," said Mildred. "He said he got $1,500.00 by it."

"There might be something to it, I suppose," said Baldwin.

"You're a government official," said Mildred. "It's your duty to do something."

Baldwin thought about it. He did not know William Trailor well. William was not a drinking man so he came in only for the rare letter he received. It did seem strange that Fisher had disappeared. If he asked the authorities to investigate and there was nothing to it, there would be no harm done. Whatever Mildred thought about him, Baldwin took the duties of the office of postmaster seriously. He knew about a possible crime; it would be irresponsible to ignore it.

"What's your interest in this?" he asked Mildred.

"I'm just doing my Christian duty as I see it," answered Mildred.

Baldwin did not believe Mildred. On the other hand he could not see that she benefited from the business. God save me from good Christian women Baldwin thought to himself.

"All right when I get a chance I'll write to the postmaster in Springfield. He should know who to tell about this."

"Thank you," said Mildred. "I knew I could count on you to do your duty. Maybe I'll stay here until you find the time so I can help you with the wording."

"Don't trouble yourself," said Baldwin.

"Don't worry," said Mildred walking to a table and sitting down solidly. She settled in with an air of finality as if she were going to take root. "I have so little to do these days that it's really no trouble at all to wait."

Baldwin puffed out his cheeks and exhaled. "I know I have a pen and ink around here somewhere."

Mildred smiled.

Chapter Ten

Friday, June 11, 1841 Springfield, Illinois

Asher Keys was a contented man. Overweight past fat, red in complexion with small brown eyes and sparse wispy mouse colored hair, he moved leisurely through the streets at an hour long past that by which most people started to work. As he walked through the streets, nodding amiably at the people he passed, he whistled a popular ditty. By dutiful political work with the Whig party (and the good luck that the last man to hold the position decided he wanted a better paying job) Keys had finally achieved his highest ambition. He was postmaster of Springfield the capitol city of the state of Illinois.

If the position did not pay much at least it did not require much in the way of duties. Mail for the whole city and the surrounding farm families came into his office. Mail going to other areas went out from his office. Since the post office was located in Keys' tavern it was usually the case that those who came to pick or drop off their mail had a drink of two before departing. That, of course, increased Keys' business and helped to make up for the low pay of the position. Keys always assured those who asked that it was the honor of the position that led to his long term campaign for the job. He smiled as he thought that his Whig party was planning another rally soon. There would be liquor in quantity to attract the thirsty populous. Politics floated on a sea of whiskey. Even at the reduced "political price" he charged his party that wouldn't hurt his business either.

Keys planned a quiet morning of reading the incoming newspapers sent to Springfield residents and chatting with his patrons about the latest gossip. Then he would go over his receipts to

71

see if the new bartender, Edwin Brown, was skimming off his profits. A better question if I'm any judge of character, Keys thought to himself, was how much the man was stealing. Brown was popular with his customers; jocular and sharp tongued so Keys hoped he was not too greedy too.

As he stepped through the door to his tavern, he automatically checked to see who was drinking and how much. From years of practice he knew at a glance just about how much money there should be in the bar till. He greeted his regular customers and inquired about their health and families. Then with a grunt, he squeezed under the bar and opened the till. The new bartender looked on uneasily.

"It was a slow morning until just before you arrived," said Brown.

"Uh," said Keys counting the coins.

"It's busier now than it has been," said Brown. "I expect it'll pick up later on."

Keys shook his head sadly. Brown, was just too greedy to keep on as bartender. Keys hated to think that he might have to get up early enough to open the bar himself. He enjoyed the unusual luxury of sleeping late and living elsewhere. Without a bartender he would not be able to wander about town and attend his political meetings. He would have to listen to the endless complaints of the chronic drinkers and he would be trapped in the tavern for hours on end.

Brown knew the signs only too well. He'd seen them before when he got fired for dipping his fingers into the till. He felt himself start to sweat. He desperately searched his mind for a way to distract Keys.

"Oh, I forgot to tell you," said Brown. "A letter came in addressed to the postmaster of Springfield. It might be important."

Privately, Brown thought Keys' political ambitions as windy and overblown as the man himself.

Keys nodded and awkwardly swung under the bar again. As Keys headed toward the post office part of the tavern, Brown mentally calculated carefully what level of bar receipts would be necessary at the end of the day to alleviate Keys suspicions. He also cursed himself for underestimating the man based only on his fat and lazy outward appearance. At the same time, Brown mentally raised his opinion of Keys. He thought to himself that he might actually come to like working for the man. Maybe, mused Brown to himself, I can learn something from Keys. He wondered what it would be like to have others think he was lazy and stupid. There certainly would be advantages to that.

Keys recognized that Brown was trying to distract him but he had seen enough to know what the man was. Besides, he was curious about the letter. In addition to more business, Keys had found that the position of postmaster brought with it a larger measure of respect than he experienced as a tavern owner. Keys found that he liked that. In turn, he tried to discharge the duties of postmaster responsibly to justify the respect.

Keys let himself into the room (which he rather grandly referred to as an office) where he kept the mail and located the letter Brown referred to. As he opened the letter, Keys tried to guess the content. As he read it, his jaw dropped open and his eyes widened. Keys rushed from the room and looked for someone to share the news with. The only men in the tavern were serious morning drinkers and the bartender. Keys barely paused before he kept moving out the door and into the street looking for an audience.

Keys nearly danced in impatience trying to think where he could go and who he could talk to. The sheriff and the state attorney general would surely be interested. Keys knew they often met together at about this time in the morning in the sheriff's office to exchange views and swap lies. He headed off in that direction at a faster speed than he had moved in years.

In the sheriff's private office across the street from the jail building Caleb Young was telling an off-color joke to the Illinois Attorney General, Josiah Lamborn. Caleb Young was a handsome, hefty, but solid man with muddy brown eyes and wavy gray-brown hair. His face was weather beaten and he had the expression of a man who has seen all the worst the world has to offer. He moved with the efficiency of a natural athlete. Josiah Lamborn was of equal height and bulk but his body was sagging rather than solid. His face was ruddy and lined. The color of his face and the prominent veins in his nose suggested his heavy use of alcohol. Lamborn had straight black hair, a nose like a hawk's beak and piercing dark brown eyes.

Both men were startled when the door flew open and Keys hurried in. Keys leaned over. He was breathing hard and unable to speak. His face was scarlet. Sheriff Young's first thought was that he had been wounded. Keys pushed the letter in his hand toward the other men insistently.

Leaving the sheriff to tend to Keys, Lamborn took the letter and read it quickly. He then read it again more slowly and carefully. Young maneuvered Keys into a chair where Keys' breathing slowed. He regained his voice.

"Ain't that the damnedest thing?" he asked Lamborn.

"Sheriff you better read this," said Lamborn handing Young the letter.

Young started to painfully decode the letter one faltering word at a time. Not unkindly, Lamborn took it from him.

"I catch crooks quicker than I catch on to written words," admitted Young."

Lamborn started to read, "Monday, June 7, 1841 Warren County, Illinois. From Alexander Baldwin, postmaster of Warren County to the postmaster of Springfield."

"Dear Sir: Recent strange and mysterious events here compel me to beg for your assistance. William Trailor, resident of this county, traveled to Springfield with Archibald Fisher, who was then boarding with his family, with the expressed purpose to visit his brother Henry Trailor in Clary's Grove and Arch Trailor of your city. I reckon he must have been in your city around the first of this month. When Mr. Trailor returned, Mr. Fisher was not with him. Mr. Trailor's explanation of the absence of Mr. Fisher leaves much unclear. It is his apparent claim that Mr. Fisher disappeared while in Springfield. We have no news of him here.

"Mr. Trailor's conduct since his return has been strange. He has refused to give an adequate explanation of what happened to Mr. Fisher. He has bought a farm paying in gold coin although he showed no such wealth before. It is believed that Mr. Fisher had wealth in the form of gold coins. In addition, it is reported that he was denounced from the pulpit of his own church, but did not respond. It is that Mr. Trailor boasted that Mr. Fisher died, willing him money and that he got about fifteen hundred dollars from it.

"We can not determine what happened here. We ask that you inform the proper authorities and desire them to investigate and ascertain what occurred. We beseech you to write us about the truth in this matter."

"Your obedient servant,

Alexander Baldwin"

"I'll be damned," said Young.

"Maybe it's not you who should be in fear of the peril to his soul," said Lamborn. "We can not allow evil of this magnitude to go unpunished."

"I need to have my deputies start on this right away," said Young. "If you gentlemen will excuse me."

"We're in your office, sheriff," said Lamborn. "We'll get out from under foot and let you have at it. Come with me Mr. Keys."

The two men left the office.

"The first thing we need to do is to get the Mayor involved," said Lamborn. "Bring your letter along and we'll see him now."

Keys felt flattered. He was seldom included in the private conversations of the political elite in town. In one morning he'd talked with the sheriff, the state attorney general and now the mayor too. Lamborn headed through the streets with a degree of energy and directness that Keys had rarely witnessed in the man before. Keys walked as quickly as he could in Lamborn's wake.

Lamborn headed toward the mayor's office never glancing back to see if Keys were following. Within a block or two Keys was breathing hard and struggling to keep pace. Fortunately for him, the mayor's office was only a short distance away.

Alvan Martin, mayor of Springfield, was practicing a speech when Lamborn came into his office with Keys following doggedly a few steps behind him. Martin was a rangy man with blond curly hair, a fair complexion and hazel eyes. He was fashionably dressed in a well fitting suit and ruffled shirt. Despite a reputation as something of a "dandy," Martin was, in truth, a master of the rough and tumble politics of the times. He was quick to use innuendo and rumor as a way accuse his opponent of whatever he thought would offend the greatest number of voters. He preferred to avoid outright accusations that could be disproved and that might eventually rebound to his detriment.

"You need to read this letter," said Lamborn.

Martin gingerly took the sweaty page from Keys and perused it carefully. He instantly realized the political advantages that would accrue to the men who were seen as bringing a murderer to justice. There were very few actions an elected official could take that did not offend someone. To bring a man to justice would bring universal approval and distract the voters from past behavior that Martin would rather not have to try to justify.

"Clearly, 'tis our civic duty to help uncover this dastardly act and punish the offender," said Martin.

"We need to organize a search for the body first," said Lamborn. "The sheriff and his deputies can't cover everywhere. Mr. Keys we need you to make copies of the letter and put them up all over town. We'll have a meeting, just after dinner, at your tavern. The mayor and I will organize all able-bodied men to conduct a thorough search of the town and of the surrounding countryside."

"I'll stand all searchers to two free drinks at my tavern," said Keys. "Well, on second thought, one free drink." Keys hurried out thinking he had more exercise that one morning than he usually did in a full week.

"That's a nice touch," said Martin. "The voters always appreciate a little excitement. Not to mention a little whiskey. If they take part in the search that we organize they'll find it very hard to turn around and vote against us at the next election."

"Elections aren't everything," said Lamborn. "We need the men of the town to find evidence so we can bring the offender to justice."

"You will admit that it's a nice bonus though," said Martin. "Why look a gift horse in the mouth?"

"How do you think the sheriff will react to the unrequested help?" asked Lamborn.

"Let me talk to him," said Martin. "He has an election coming up, himself. Surely someone will run against him. I had thought of putting up a shadow candidate myself but I've reached no firm conclusion about the possible benefits of a change in the office."

"At least Mr. Lincoln is out of town on the court circuit," said Lamborn. "That should make it easier for us to get folks stirred up."

"I still say you make too much out of that undereducated back woods boy," said Martin.

"I've contended against Mr. Lincoln in the courtroom," said Lamborn. "You have not. I warn you not to underestimate him."

Friday June 11, 1841 Danville, Illinois

Abraham Lincoln stood with his arms crossed rocking back and forth slightly looking quizzically at the man on the witness stand.

"Let me see if I can get to the bottom of this," said Lincoln. "You admit, Mr. Smith, that you were the one who opened the ball by attacking my client, Mr. White. Is that correct?"

Smith looked in the direction of his attorney.

"Answer the question," barked Judge Davis

"Um, yes sir," answered Smith.

"After you attacked Mr. White, he beat you like a drum. Didn't he?"

"Yes sir," answered Smith.

"You hit him when he was not even looking at you but he turned around and he cleaned your plow, right?"

The men in the jury smiled and chuckled openly.

"Yes sir," answered Smith in a small voice.

"What was that again? I'm not sure that I heard you," said Lincoln.

"Yes sir," said Smith.

"And then after you could not beat him in a fight when you threw the first punch you took him to court charging assault and battery hoping to win here what you could not manage to win on your own."

"Objection, your honor," said Smith's attorney.

"I find Mr. Smith's behavior objectionable too," said Lincoln.

"Your honor," started Smith's attorney.

"I apologize," said Lincoln. "I meant no disrespect to the court."

Lincoln turned to the jury. "It's just that my client found himself in a position like the man who was walking along a country road with a pitchfork over his shoulder. A farmer's vicious dog came out of a barn and attacked the man. In defending himself the man stuck out the pitchfork and in parrying off the dog the brute became impaled on the prongs and died.

The farmer asked, "What made you kill my dog?"

The man answered, "What made him attack me?"

The farmer asked, "Why didn't you defend yourself with the other end of the pitchfork?"

The man answered, "Why didn't your dog come at me with his other end?"

Lincoln whirled an imaginary dog in his long arms and jabbed at the jury with the imaginary dog's extended tail. In short order the jury acquitted Lincoln's client of the assault and battery charge.

Chapter Eleven

Friday June 11, 1841 Springfield, Illinois

Keys' tavern was not large enough to hold all the excited, restless men who assembled there after dinner. Opinions were expressed with vehemence and certainty. Tobacco was smoked and chewed (and spit.) Keys noted with pleasure the number of men who had a drink to follow the one he offered "on the house." He made certain that Brown saw him assessing the size of the crowd and the number of drinks poured. After the morning's adventure, he felt more forgiving. He thought he might just keep Brown on as bartender, if the man showed that he knew enough to leave most of the take in the till.

Most of the men in the crowd seemed cheerful. They joked with one another and boasted about their strength or their horses. They clearly enjoyed the chance to escape from the dreary daily grind of hard work and unending responsibility. The crowd had the good natured rowdy feel of a group of boys playing hooky on a dare.

Martin and Lamborn climbed up on a table to get everyone's attention. "Gentlemen, gentlemen," said Martin in his practiced speaking voice that carried throughout the room. "Let's get started."

After some good-tempered jeering, crowd quieted down somewhat. Privately, Keys was pleased to note that traffic to the bar seemed unaffected.

"You've had a chance to read the letter from the postmaster of Warren County," said Lamborn. "You know that foul murder was committed in this city. As a civilized society, we can not allow this to pass unavenged. I am gratified to see how many civic-minded men are here to defend the ideals under which we all live. I thank you for your efforts, in advance of the event."

"Under the laws of Illinois we must find the body to be able to be certain of a conviction of unlawful murder. Therefore, the first task we undertake must be to discover where the body was hidden. We can assume the lawbreaker exercised a certain level cunning since the body has not yet been discovered by accident. Still, with a concerted effort, we should be able to pull back the curtain of this crime and uncover what has been concealed from our view."

The crowd cheered. Men had the heady feeling that they were cheering for themselves.

"With the help of the sheriff we have devised a pattern of search that covers the city and it's environs completely," said Martin. "We will divide into regiments with each group to choose a captain and as many lieutenants as needed. The state attorney general and I will coordinate efforts and compile information. We will be centered here."

Martin held up a large map divided into sections. The men crowded forward to get a better view.

"If you find something do not touch it or move it," said Lamborn. "Send a runner back here so the sheriff and I can investigate further. It is equally important that, when you complete a search of an area and you do not find anything, send someone back with that information too. Then we will not waste time re-searching a place that has been examined before."

"Some of the search will be unpleasant," warned Martin. "By this time, the body will have begun moldering. As you know, the process of decay is vile to see, and smell."

Some of the men looked concerned and turned to speak with their neighbors. The men on the table waited for the noise to subside.

"Some areas of search will include graveyards where freshly dug graves will have to be disturbed and bodies will have to be disinterred," said Lamborn. "This will not disturb the immortal souls of the dearly departed, which are safely in heaven, but it will be disturbing to the searchers. We will ask for those searchers to be strong of will, mind, and stomach."

A louder and more sustained muttering followed that announcement. Some men looked uneasily at their neighbors. They knew that any man who reacted with timidity or loathing could expect to be mercilessly taunted by those who did not. A number of men concluded silently that they should avoid joining the groups covering graveyards.

"Some people may object to the search," said Martin. "Tell them to talk with the sheriff, the attorney general, or me. It is a necessary search to apprehend the law breaker."

"What if we don't find anything?" asked Ignatius Langford. He was a mason and bricklayer. With black hair and eyes and a massive frame, Langford appeared as strong and unmoving as the stones he worked with, but his temper sparked as easily as flint struck with steel.

"Then we'll keep searching until we do," answered Lamborn.

The men cheered again. With jokes and jockeying to avoid some men and to join others, the assignments were made and the assembled men elected their leaders. Lamborn and Martin quietly made certain that each group included some men who were both sober and responsible. Kelly, the whiskey seller, tried to influence his group by buying free drinks to all who would promise to vote for him, but the men in his group accepted the drinks and then voted for

Manasseh Porter, the hostler. Kelly's angry responses were thought to be hilarious by the men of the group.

Keys, in a magnanimous gesture, decided to let Brown accompany the regiment in which Ignatius Langford was captain. He manned the bar himself and took charge of the moneybox. During the afternoon negative reports trickled back to the tavern. Ditches, wells, cellars, pits, and crevices of all sorts were examined, inch-by-inch.

To his surprise, Elijah Hart, the drayman was elected lieutenant under Captain Leonard James, the blacksmith. Their group dug up a recently buried horse, and then a big dog. The bodies were partly putrid. The smell and appearance of the bodies greatly decreased the enthusiasm of the men in the platoon. One man, who had imbibed entirely too much of Keys' whiskey, noisomely emptied his stomach on the ground nearby which only added to the stench.

James refused to let the men abandon the search and Hart backed him up. None of the men wanted to face up to the muscular blacksmith let alone the combination of the blacksmith and the wiry drayman together. As short as Hart was, he drove a team of massive workhorses and moved heavy objects for many hours each day. Fortunately, the area to be searched did not include any additional graves.

Still, as the hot afternoon wore on the alcohol based "Dutch courage" of some of the men wore off. There were an increasing number of searchers who had second thoughts about the entire enterprise. The men searched huts and hovels, buildings under construction, and abandoned buildings that threatened to fall down around their ears. Men began to remember pressing business that they had forgotten before. They began to mutter among themselves about the heat and the work. Just before dinnertime James carefully marked the progress they had made on his map. He set the time and place of assembly for tomorrow, sent a runner to Keys' tavern to share with them the progress that had been made, and sent the rest of the men to their home for the night.

Dinner at the Myers was strained and uncomfortable that night.

Arch Trailor was angry and upset that his brother was suspected of murder.

"I don't see how the mayor and the attorney general can think that William would do anything like that," said Arch.

"They don't know your brother like you do," said Mrs. Myers.

"There wasn't a thing in the letter but gossip and old wives tales," insisted Arch. I know William has had hard currency for years. He even gave me a gold piece when I left home. He just doesn't see any reason to talk about it. Why should he? If he decided to buy a farm with coin, is that illegal?"

"You have to admit, that he left here without Mr. Fisher and without leaving him a way to get home," said Kelly. "I told him not to do that."

Arch threw down his napkin and stood up facing Kelly. Arch's muscles were tense and his face was flushed. "Just what is that supposed to mean?"

"Nothing," said Kelly meekly. "I was just saying it was strange."

"Do you know why the searchers found nothing today?" asked Arch. "It's because there's nothing out there to find. They can search for a year, or ten years, and there will still be nothing to find."

"Then you have nothing to worry about," said Dutch. "Please sit down."

Dinner continued with very little conversation. Arch finished dinner quickly and went outside to be by himself. Mrs. Myers looked at Kelly coldly for the rest of the meal. After the table was cleared Mrs. Myers talked with Dutch.

"I wish I could help him," said Mrs. Myers.

"So do I," said Dutch. "But I think at the moment he wants to be alone with his thoughts."

"How terrible it must be to have your own brother accused of murder," said Mrs. Myers.

"Yes," said Dutch. "It is a good thing that William Trailor is no longer in this town. There are already men talking about a hanging."

"You don't think anyone would try to hurt Arch do you?" asked Mrs. Myers.

"So far there is no talk about anyone except William," said Dutch. "People know Arch and they like him. They'd have a hard time thinking he would kill someone. William is a stranger. He's far away. It's easier to talk when you don't have to back up what you say with action."

"But if they get liquored up and William is not available, who knows what may happen," said Mrs. Myers. "I don't like the ugly mood of the town. There are a few men spoiling for a hanging. Right now it is only a few but it will spread. It's like a fever that gets into the blood. A man may catch it from one man and pass it on to another."

"I know," said Dutch. "There is nothing we can do. It's time to go to bed."

"I wish that Mr. Lincoln was not out of town riding the court circuit." Mrs. Myers said. "I would feel more at my ease if I could talk to him."

"He might know what could be done," agreed Dutch. "I do not."

Arch sat alone in the darkness for a long time.

Chapter Twelve

Saturday June 12, 1841 Springfield, Illinois

Early the next morning the men met again at Keys' tavern. Keys noted that this morning he sold more coffee and food than whiskey. Although there were fewer men than the day before, they seemed more serious and determined than the day before.

Lamborn entered the tavern and quietly talked with some of the men. He nailed a large map of the city and the surrounding area on the wall. Large sections were covered with hatch marks.

"You can see that we made considerable progress yesterday," said Lamborn. "We can eliminate areas already covered from today's search."

Lamborn noted the serious mood in the room.

"I am glad that you gentlemen take this seriously. What we are looking for is not the result of a killing by misadventure. It was not drunken brawl that ended in tragedy. It was not even a long simmering feud that blew up unexpectedly. What we are looking for is evidence of a cold blooded, carefully planned execution for the purpose of obtaining money. The hiding place may have been as cunningly thought out as the murder obviously was."

Martin slipped into the room as Lamborn continued to speak.

"I am pleased that so many of you responsible citizens are determined not to let the murderer slip through our fingers."

Martin walked over to Keys at the bar. He noted that the men in the room were gathered around Lamborn and that there was no one at the bar. "I'll wager our Mr. Lamborn has rarely had the opportunity to practice his opening argument for the court with members of the jury before the trail even starts." said Martin.

"I never thought of that," said Keys. "You're right these men are the one who serve on juries. You think Mr. Trailor will be arrested and tried then."

"Of course," said Martin. "What other outcome could there be?"

"We will continue as yesterday using the same regiments and officers," said Lamborn to the crowd. "I see there are nearly as many men here today as there were yesterday. I have new assignments for groups that finished their areas. For the rest of you continue from where you stopped in the area you had. When you finish that you can report back here."

Brown, the bartender, raised his voice. "I've heard talk that the Trailors were seen to have a lot of gold pieces."

Brown was pleased to note the excited murmur that followed his announcement. His statement was based on the ruminations of a few, bitter late night drunks overheard at the bar. He hoped the outpouring of interest in his statement would help solidify his place in the affections of Keys' customers. That would make it harder for Keys to get rid of him when the final reckoning over the cash box came about.

"I heard that he paid the livery stable in gold," shouted one man.

"That's not so," said Manasseh Porter who was the hostler at the livery. His response was lost in the noise of the crowd.

"I heard that he paid for his board in gold," insisted another.

"The last time Henry Trailor was in town he was boasting at the tavern about how rich he was," said Ignatius Langford "I heard him myself."

"Last night at supper Arch Trailor bragged that he got gold from his older brother," said Kelly.

"That's a lie!" shouted James. For a moment the crowd was quiet. "Dennis Kelly, you take that back right now or step outside and answer to me. I was there. What Arch said was that when he moved to Springfield years ago William gave him one gold coin."

"Mr. James is right," said Hart. "I was there too. Kelly is a liar. If you don't want to have a go at Mr. James, Mr. Kelly, you can try me on for size. I may be half the size of the blacksmith but I'm man enough to skin you and nail your hide to the barn."

Kelly eyes darted around the room as if seeking an escape. His eyes blinked rapidly.

"Maybe...maybe," said Kelly, "I misunderstood what Arch said. He was pretty hot at the time."

"That's not good enough," said James. "Arch wasn't hot and you're still lying."

"Now that I think about it," said Kelly slowly, "Arch did say he got the gold piece years ago."

Most of the men looked at Kelly with contempt. A few seemed disappointed that there would not be a thrashing. In a few moments the men in the tavern began to joke and argue once again. The noise rose back to its previous level.

"I've never seen three brothers hung together," said Martin to Keys quietly. "It should be quite a sight."

"But Kelly admitted he lied," said Keys.

"He planted the seed all the same," said Martin. "I'll wager it bears fruit."

"You think there will a hanging?" asked Keys.

"I'd be mighty surprised if there isn't at least one," said Martin.

"Hey!" exclaimed Lamborn to the assembled men. "It damn near got exciting here."

The men laughed.

"Now that's over let's get to work and nail the murderer," said Lamborn.

In good spirits the men moved out to continue the search.

James worked his way over to Kelly.

"I'll help you move your things to a new boarding house," James said to Kelly.

"But, but, I don't want to move."

"I'll help too," said Hart putting his hand on Kelly's shoulder and squeezed, exerting more force than was absolutely necessary. Kelly winced but remained silent.

The search continued methodically throughout the morning but yielded no more than the earlier search had. Root cellars, empty lots and drainage ditches all proved to be free of unexplained bodies. The area left to be searched diminished slowly with no positive result. At dinnertime the searchers broke for the meal.

Martin and Lamborn examined the map over a meal in Keys' tavern.

"We're nearly out of territory," said Martin. "No bodies so far."

"It probably won't turn up after this amount of time," said Lamborn. "The search needed to be made but all along the chances were that the body was dumped in a creek or buried so far out in the woods that it'll never be found."

"Can you prosecute the crime without a body?" asked Martin.

"Oh, I can prosecute it," said Lamborn. "A better question is — Can I get a conviction without a body?"

"Do you think you can?" said asked Martin.

"That, my friend, is an excellent question."

Lamborn laced his finger together and rested his chin on his hands. He sat in silence for a moment.

"If I can not have a body, I would settle for a confession. If nothing turns up this afternoon, or even if it does, I'll ask the sheriff to send his deputies to arrest William and Henry Trailor," said Lamborn.

As Lamborn expected the afternoon yielded no positive result. The searchers went home to supper. Lamborn met with Martin and Caleb Young, the sheriff.

"We need to compare results and make plans," said Lamborn. "Why don't you start first, sheriff?"

"All right," said Young. "My deputies and I backtracked all three Trailors and Mr. Fisher from the time they came into town until when the second brother, Henry, left the second time. I took Arch through the whole thing, of course, and the deputies or I checked what he said against what other witnesses saw. So far what Arch said holds up in every detail."

"You would say that Arch is a credible witness, then?" asked Lamborn.

"Definitely," said Young. "He's a hard working young man and he's well respected. Anyway, I can track the four men through dinner and afterward as they walk around the town. They see the sights. They stop by Ward's Carriage builders' shop. The Trailors head off without Mr. Fisher. Then Mr. Fisher disappears."

Young shook his head in wonder. "I can't find anybody who saw Mr. Fisher after the Trailors left him in front of the carriage shop," said Young. "I've got him tracked that far by various witnesses. I've even got a bunch of boys who looked at the model carriage with him. They saw the Trailors leave. Then they go off to play and Mr. Fisher vanishes."

"Did the boys say that the Trailors spoke to Mr. Fisher when they left?" asked Lamborn.

"Yes," said Young. "The old man (that's what they called William) said they'd meet him at supper. When he didn't show up the Trailors talked about it with the other boarders."

"The boarders were bound to notice Mr. Fisher's absence on their own," said Lamborn. "If you were setting up an alibi, you would want to bring the matter up yourself first. Did the Trailors claim to search for him?"

"The Trailors went out, supposedly to search for him," said Young, "after dinner and then after supper on the first day. They asked the other boarders to keep an eye peeled for him but they didn't ask them to join the search. The next day before breakfast and after breakfast until dinner they searched again. Arch talked to Jim Maxey at my office then. After dinner William and Henry left to head home. Mr. Kelly protested that they'd not even made the rounds of the taverns with him and that Mr. Fisher would not have a way home."

"So, Mr. Kelly can testify that he objected to William going off and leaving Mr. Fisher without a way to get back home but William left anyway," said Lamborn.

"Yes," answered Young, "For whatever his testimony is worth. He comes across as a shady customer. I don't know what a jury would think of him."

Martin said, "Two men called him a liar to his face today. He didn't deny it or fight for his honor. Also, he doesn't seem to much like Arch."

"You've got to take the witnesses you've got," said Lamborn. "I've been stuck with worse than him before."

"Was that all the searching that was done?" asked Martin.

"No," said Young. "Henry returned a few days later. He, some friends, and Arch got the boarders, and some men who knew Mr. Fisher from Warren County, to look with them with no result. At one time or another they talked to doctors, horse traders, bartenders, my deputy, people Mr. Fisher might have known from Warren County, passers by and store clerks. They also put an advertisement in the Illinois State Register and the Sangamo Journal."

"That's just what I'd do if I were covering my back trail," said Lamborn. "Maybe it's a case of – 'Me think thou dost protest too much.' You notice how long it was before the brothers allowed the boarders to get actively involved in the search. They had the time and the opportunity to kill Mr. Fisher, to conceal the body and then to move it. It could have been hidden anywhere."

"When Jim Maxey spoke with Arch," said Young, "he thought the young man was genuinely concerned. Jim brought up the idea that Mr. Fisher might be dead and Arch seemed shocked. Jim's seen a lot of flummery and flash in his time. He'd be a hard man to bamboozle."

"The older brothers might not have involved Arch in their plot," said Lamborn. "What a perfect cover it would be to leave the youngest innocent. Arch is known and respected here. He'd be likely to deflect any inquiry without even knowing that he was acting as a cover for his brothers' crimes. That's brilliant. It's just the sort of thing a really intelligent murderer might do."

"I know one thing," said Martin. "I'm glad you didn't decide on a life of crime, Mr. attorney general."

"Who says I didn't?" asked Lamborn.

The men laughed.

"Did you learn about anything unusual that the Trailors did while they were in town?" asked Lamborn.

"They talked with Abraham Lincoln," said Young. "Henry lives near an old friend of his."

"Maybe they were short on tall tales," said Martin.

The men laughed again.

"When William and Henry left town they left by a road to the northwest that did not lead to their homes," said Young. "It went into the woods. They were seen back in town about an hour later.

Then they left by the road to the northwest that did lead to their homes."

"Interesting," said Lamborn. "Let's look at the map."

The men walked over to the wall and examined the map hanging there.

"Here's where the search has gone so far," said Martin pointing to the marked areas of the map. "The searchers haven't found any unaccounted for bodies, no bloody clothes, no signs of a struggle, no discarded weapons, nothing."

"This crime was committed, intelligently" said Lamborn. "So the weapon could have been some object we would not normally think of as a weapon at all. Maybe it was a rock or a board. Maybe it was a chisel or a rolling pin."

"I know," said Martin. "It's what you would have done if you committed the crime. If any more clues like this come up I'm going to accuse you."

Young and Martin laughed. Lamborn looked serious.

"Back to the matter at hand," said Lamborn, "The searchers have not yet covered the area northwest of Springfield. That might be the next area that should investigated."

"Once the woods start, there is no way to completely examine the ground," said Young. "Although it would be a good place to discard a body."

"Like I told Martin, I don't really expect to find much more evidence," said Lamborn. "The murder was too carefully planned and carried out to leave many traces. I'd like your deputies to pick up William and Henry. I want to sweat them about the crime."

"All right," said Young. "I don't think you have enough information right now for a successful prosecution."

"I'd like you to send Mr. Wickersham to pick up Henry tomorrow," said Lamborn. "I want to talk to him first about what he is to say and how he is to act."

"Jim Maxey is a better deputy," said Young. "Mr. Wickersham has not been a deputy for long and he's a sight younger than Mr. Maxey."

"I know," said Lamborn. "That's why I want him to pick up the man behind the whole thing — William Trailor. William has sons in the area who might object. Mr. Maxey will bring him in whatever happens."

"Jim could also bring in any witnesses who have seen him throwing gold coins around, the postmaster and other relevant witnesses," said Young. "He has a way of uncovering things."

"He has a way of doing things on his own too," said Lamborn. "I don't think William will admit anything to anybody. He's likely to act the innocent whatever happens but maybe we can persuade Henry to cooperate. Mr. Maxey is a good officer but Mr. Wickersham will be better for what we need him to do. He follows orders without asking why."

"What about Arch?" asked Martin.

"We'll leave him alone for the moment at least," said Lamborn. "We can shear that sheep later if need be."

Saturday June 12, 1841 Danville, Illinois

Abraham Lincoln sat in a borrowed law office facing a woman of middle years dressed in a calico dress and bonnet.

"I appreciate you taking the time to look over my settlement, Mr. Lincoln," said Mrs. Brown. "It is hard for me as a widow to know if the land bequest is correct."

"I'm happy to do it," said Lincoln. "The circuit court is in recess until Monday so I have little enough to occupy my time. I am also happy to be able to tell you that the bequest was fully met by your neighbors. In fact there was an error in your favor. They deeded you three acres more than you were due. Neither your neighbors nor the land office clerk are aware of the mistake. How would you care to address it?"

"What do you mean?" asked Mrs. Brown.

"Do you prefer to have the deed corrected and give up the land or would you rather offer them the going price for the three additional acres? I've seen the land and it looks prime to me if you have the capitol to pay for it. If you call it to your neighbors' attention and offer a fair price I'd predict that they will sell it to you happily and praise you as a honest woman to boot."

"It would be wrong to profit from the errors of others," said Mrs. Brown. "Wouldn't it? Do you happen to know the going rate for an acre, Mr. Lincoln?"

"It happens that I do."

Chapter Thirteen

Sunday June 13, 1841 on the road toward Clary's Grove, Illinois early in the morning

Jim Maxey and Alonzo Wickersham rode together toward Clary's Grove. Wickersham was a big young man with long curly brown hair and a short beard. His eyes were as black as obsidian and he had a toothy smile. People often compared him to a bear. He rode a quick-footed horse and he often rode ahead of Maxey for a while before dropping back to keep the older man company.

"I don't know why you ride so slow," said Wickersham.

"I've got a far piece to go," said Maxey. "Much farther than you do. I'll get there and back again a lot sooner if I set a reasonable pace than if I go racing off and wear my horse down."

"Do you think the Trailors will resist arrest?" asked Wickersham.

"It's not likely Henry will," said Maxey. "He's got a wife, a small child, and baby with him. He'll likely be scared out of his mind."

"What about William?" asked Wickersham.

"That could be different but I doubt it," said Maxey. "I'm not expecting trouble."

"But you're prepared if trouble happens," said Wickersham.

"I'll bring him back if that's what you're asking," said Maxey.

"I have special instructions about what to do with Henry," said Wickersham. "I'm not supposed to talk about them."

"That's probably for the best," answered Maxey. "You can't be too careful. There are already rumors all over town about the Trailors. If they spent all the gold they're supposed to have spent they must be related to King Midas."

"I'm sure Mr. Lamborn didn't mean I couldn't talk to you about it," said Wickersham. "Hell, we're both deputies."

"Is Mr. Lamborn giving instructions now?" asked Maxey.

"Didn't he talk to you?" asked Wickersham.

"No," said Maxey. "Only the sheriff talked to me."

"Mr. Lamborn is a mighty smart man," said Wickersham. "He figured thing out who committed the murder without much information from the search. He's determined that they will be punished for it."

"He's a like a bulldog," said Maxey. "Once he gets his teeth into an idea he won't let it go. He purely hates criminals."

"That's a man who knows how criminals should be treated too," said Wickersham. "He won't mollycoddle anybody."

"I'd hate to have him think I committed a crime," said Maxey.

"You wouldn't commit a crime," protested Wickersham.

"I'm certainly not planning on it," answered Maxey with a smile.

"If I did anything I'd hate to have you on my trail. Mr. Lamborn may be a bulldog, but you're a blue tick bloodhound."

"Why thank you, Alonzo. To tell you the truth if you did something wrong I'd hate to have to bring you back. I would, of course, but I'd sorely regret it."

"Do you think the Trailors will hang?" asked Wickersham. "Mr. Lamborn does. I think Mr. Martin does too."

"I don't think Arch had anything to do with it," said Maxey. "As to the other two, that's for the jury to decide. We bring them in. Mr. Lamborn prosecutes them. The jury does the final judging."

"I can't figure Mr. Lamborn," said Wickersham. "He's cold as steel when it comes to outlaws, but any old bummer with a sad story can count on him for enough money for a meal and a place to sleep. Besides, as smart as he is, he can't put down the whiskey bottle until it's empty. He knows where that path leads but he can't get off it."

"No man is all of one piece," said Maxey. "I've known honest thieves and merciful killers. There are preachers who have no forgiveness in them and sinners who know more about God than most clergymen."

"The men who committed this murder," said Wickersham. "I mean, the way they figured out when to kill without being seen and how to get rid of the body without a trace, they had to plan it out ahead of time, like carpenters planning out a building on paper, or a farmer reckoning when and what to plant as crops. Those men have to be as cold as ice in January. Don't you think?"

"It would seem that way," answered Lamborn.

"So they wouldn't deserve being handled like cracked egg shell would they?" asked Wickersham.

"Just as long as what you do is legal," said Lamborn. "Don't go making up things the man didn't say. Don't assault the man. One of the differences between us and them is that we go by the rules. Your personal integrity is worth more than a conviction any time. Even if other people don't know you've lied you will. Even if you know a man to be guilty, it'll eat at your respect for your own self like strong acid etches glass."

"I'll keep that in mind," said Wickersham. "Thank you."

"You're welcome," said Maxey.

The two men rode along in contemplative but companionable silence for a time. They came to a fork in the road.

"Here's where we part company," said Wickersham. "I guess I don't need to tell you what Mr. Lamborn said after all. I'll be back in Springfield before you."

"I'll see you there," said Maxey. He rode on alone keeping a steady pace and thinking about the attorney general and the corrosive effects of acid.

Wickersham urged his horse into a faster trot along the road. He had only a general knowledge of the area so he hoped to meet someone to get exact direction to Henry Trailor's farm. In the distance he heard a regular series of sharp thumps. He followed the sound and discovered a man in a field next to the road chopping firewood for loading into his wagon. The woodchopper was a hefty man of early middle years. He had black hair streaked with white and a salt and pepper beard. The man moved with efficiency and his chopping appeared effortless. He had an air of physical competence. Wickersham thought to himself: If people compare me to a bear, this man is a he grizzly.

"Howdy," called Wickersham.

The man looked up from his work. "Howdy," he replied. He started to pick up the smaller pieces of wood and put them into the wagon.

"Can I help?" asked Wickersham. He dismounted and approached the man.

"If you've a mind to," said the man.

Wickersham picked up wood and helped to load the wagon. He noticed that, although the man was shorter than Wickersham, he was more heavily built. Each time that Wickersham increased the load he lifted and put in the wagon, the man made his load even heavier. Soon Wickersham was staggering under the weight of wood but the man carried even heavier loads without apparent effort.

Neither man spoke as they loaded the wagon. Wickersham was sweating and straining. He had little breath left for conversation. The man seemed content to work without making a sound. Finally the wagon was full and Wickersham sank to the ground.

"Thank you kindly," said the man. "You're a lawman. Who are you hunting?"

"How did you know?" asked Wickersham.

"From the smell," said the man without smiling.

Wickersham wondered if that was a joke.

"In my younger days I had some run ins with the law," said the man. "I learned to tell."

"Well, you're right," said Wickersham. "I'm Alonzo Wickersham, a deputy from Springfield. I'll own I'm new to the trade. I'm here to arrest Henry Trailor."

"You work hard, for a deputy," said the man. "Likely you'll stop working if you ever get to be sheriff. I'm Jack Armstrong. You can ride along next to the wagon. Where I'm heading I'll pass by close to the Trailor place."

"I've heard of you from Mr. Lincoln," said Wickersham.

"Is he still claiming he won that fight?" asked Armstrong. "I cleaned his plow for him. Although I'll allow that he was the best fighter I ever knew excepting myself."

"He tells quite a story about it," said Wickersham.

"He never tells it the same way twice I bet," said Armstrong. "I asked him why that was once and he said he didn't want to bore himself."

"Thank you for showing me the way to Mr. Trailor's place," said Wickersham.

"You're welcome," said Armstrong. "I don't guess it matters to you that he's not the kind of man who'd kill another man, like he's supposed to done. Oh yes, we hear the wild tales up this way too."

"My job is to arrest him and take him back," said Wickersham. "The jury will decide if he's guilty or not."

Armstrong climbed up on his wagon and Wickersham remounted his horse.

"You already talk like a law man," said Armstrong. They rode along in an uneasy truce.

"You follow that path over the hills," said Armstrong. "When you get to a stream, go downstream for about a mile. You'll come to a fence. Follow that to the west and you'll come to the farmhouse. I want you to make a promise to me, Wickersham. When you get back to Springfield, you'll hunt up Abraham Lincoln and tell him about this. The Trailors will need all the help they can get."

"I promise," said Wickersham. He followed Armstrong's directions and in a short time he saw the smoke from Henry Trailor's chimney. He paused for a moment when the farmhouse first came into view. Then he swallowed, squared his shoulders, and kicked his horse lightly. Wickersham rode up to the house. He saw no movement although the chimney continued to smoke. Wickersham dismounted and strode to the door. He pounded on the door repeatedly with his fist, which sent sound booming through the house.

In a few moments Henry came to the door. His feet were bare. His hair was mused. He was tucking his shirt into his pants.

"What's wrong?" Henry asked.

"Henry Trailor?" asked Wickersham.

"I, yes I am," answered Henry.

"I've come for you," said Wickersham. "You're under arrest. You'll be coming back to Springfield with me."

"Wh-What for?" asked Henry.

"For the murder of Archibald Fisher," said Wickersham.

Henry groaned aloud and looked like he would collapse to the floor. Unsteady on his feet, Henry sat down on the floor to avoid falling. Hattie Trailor, a slight pretty blond woman dressed in an old dress and carrying an infant in her arms, approached.

"Henry, what's wrong?"

"I'm sorry, Ma'am," said Wickersham. "I'm a deputy from Springfield and I've been sent to arrest your husband for the murder of Archibald Fisher."

Hattie abruptly sat on the floor and burst into tears. The baby started to shriek. A small boy came into the room, ran to his parents and started wailing. Wickersham stood in the doorway uncertain of what to do. Finally, feeling foolish, he sat down on the floor next to the family and waited.

Henry Trailor was the first to recover. "There must be a mistake," he insisted. "I don't know what happened to Mr. Fisher but I surely didn't kill him."

"I don't know about that, sir," said Wickersham. "You'll have to get ready and come back with me." Wickersham rose to his feet.

"But its Sunday," wailed Hattie standing up and pulling on Wickersham's coat like small child pulling on her father. "We haven't gone to church yet. You wouldn't take a man from his family on the Sabbath would you?"

Thinking of his instructions Wickersham hardened his heart and replied. "No Ma'am. I would not. I don't know how many more Sabbaths you will have together."

Tears began to pour from Hattie's eyes. Wickersham winced at the sight.

"Oh thank you, kind sir," said Hattie.

Then Wickersham felt even worse.

"Come with me, dear," said Hattie to Henry. "We'll dress for church."

Hattie reached down to her husband who was still sitting on the floor. Henry reached up and allowed himself to be pulled erect. He stumbled off behind Hattie. The small boy looked up at Wickersham reproachfully. Then he too walked after his parents. Wickersham stood in the doorway uncertainly. Would Henry come back with a gun? Was he in danger of his life? He thought about what Maxey said and felt somewhat better. It would not do, he thought, to have the Trailors come back and find him indecisively holding his hat in his hand. Wickersham moved into the room and sat at the dinner table facing the direction the Trailors gone.

Inside their room the Trailors conversed in fierce whispers.

"God damn that old man," said Wickersham. Whether he was referring to Fisher or William was not clear.

"I hardly think this is the time to take the Lord's name in vain," said Hattie.

"What are we going to do?" asked Henry. He thought wildly of getting a gun or slipping out the window.

"We will go to church," said Hattie. "That's what we'll do. We're going to ask God to see us throughout this time of darkness and to protect us from evil."

She efficiently changed Abigail and supervised Adam getting dressed.

"You told me that Mr. Fisher disappeared," Hattie said, "You didn't know how or why."

"That's right."

Adam brought in a shirt for his mother's approval and she shook her head negatively.

107

"Did you brothers know anything about it?" she asked.

Henry hesitated. "I don't think so."
"William left Springfield without Mr. Fisher," said Hattie.

Adam brought in a pair of shoes that met with his mother's positive nod.

"Yes," said Henry, "After searching for two days turned up nothing. He had a farm and a family to get back to, after all."

"It sounds suspicious," said Hattie.

"It sounds suspicious," agreed Henry. "Now when Mr. Fisher hasn't turned up and accusations are flying. Back when it happened nobody thought anything about it."

"You were not with your brothers every single second," insisted Hattie. "You told me that you bought the ribbons and thread I wanted by yourself. You said William encouraged you to do it on you own. That was just after Mr. Fisher was last seen. After shopping you didn't see your brothers for a time. You don't know what they did when they were out of your sight."

Adam came into the room and Hattie absently began to comb his hair.

"They don't know what I did when I was out of their sight either," said Henry.

"That's one of the things I worry about," said Hattie.

"What do you mean?" asked Henry.

"You don't know what they might say to protect themselves," said Hattie.

"I still know what you mean,"

108

"I'm just thinking out loud," said Hattie. "I don't mean anything."

Hattie inspected Adam critically and wiped his face with a wet cloth. Henry, still feeling shaky, dressed slowly in the suit he wore to church services. When the rest of her family was dressed Hattie quickly completed her own preparations while Henry got together things for Abigail at Hattie's direction. When the Trailors reentered the front room they found Wickersham seated comfortably at the dinning room table.

"You folks look real nice," said Wickersham. He rose with his hat in his hand. "Can I help you hitch the team?" he asked.

Henry responded with a jerky nod. He and Wickersham went out to the barn and hitched the team to a small wagon. Henry looked wistfully at the pitchfork and the shovel hanging on the wall of the barn.

"Don't go do anything foolish," advised Wickersham. "I'd purely hate to have to kill you in front of your family."

Henry flinched, as if he had been struck, but said nothing.

When the men brought the wagon out of the barn Hattie climbed on carrying Abigail. Adam climbed up carefully carrying a bag full of baby supplies.

"Are you coming with us?" asked Hattie politely but coldly.

Yes Ma'am," answered Wickersham. "I think I'll ride my horse so you folks have more room in the wagon."

"Do you think we're all going to try to escape together?" Hattie asked less politely. "Two adults with a small boy and a baby?"

109

"No Ma'am," replied Wickersham. "I just reckon it would do me no harm to listen to a preacher this Sunday."

Wickersham hesitated. "I also don't believe in leaving a man open to temptation to run when I don't have to."

"There's no need to be insulting," said Henry.

"I'm just being honest, Mr. Trailor," said Henry. "I wouldn't want to go back to the sheriff and tell him I let you drive away without following. If you were in my position, you wouldn't let a man under arrest drive away out of your sight either."

Wickersham followed the wagon to a small building that from the layout he decided served as a tavern at other times. People dressed in their good clothes stood around looking at him intently. Wickersham decided that Jack Armstrong had already informed his neighbors about why he was there. In a small community gossip traveled faster than the wind. At some sign Wickersham did not detect the people filed into the rough structure. Wickersham stayed in the back in hopes of drawing as little attention as possible. An awkward young man dressed in a wrinkled black broadcloth suit approached the center of the room and cleared his throat.

"I see we have a visitor," the minister said indicating Wickersham. "I'm certain you all know why he is here."

There was an unfriendly murmur from the congregation.

"Friends, friends," said the minister holding up his hands, "this man is only doing his job. We cannot criticize him even if he is here to take away one of our own. As Christians we should pray that he sees the error of his ways."

For one of the few times in his life, Wickersham wished he were smaller and less conspicuous. He tried to shrink into the seat.

The minister seemed to be totally unacquainted with the concept of forgiveness. He preached a lesson of resisting evil and not bending to Godless authority. He cited verses about Daniel escaping from the lion's den. He talked about the Israelites throwing off their bondage in Egypt and becoming a free people. He spoke of prisoners casting off their chains. With each biblical example he looked at Wickersham piercingly. Even the hymns the minister selected were about the same sort of thing. By the end of the service Wickersham thought the congregation would rise up in a body and attack him. But that did not happen. Finally the service was over. People streamed over to the Trailors to offer words of encouragement and support. The women chattered and exclaimed about the baby while the men shook Henry's hand or pounded him on the back.

Except for dirty looks Wickersham was ignored. After the last person headed for the door, the Trailors slowly and unwillingly started to gather their belongings together. Henry and Hattie took their time at rounding up Adam and picking up Abigail. Wickersham recognized that they felt safe where they were but that the illusion of safety was fragile. He waited patiently saying nothing and not hurrying them.

Finally, out of excuses not to move, Henry and Hattie headed toward the door. The minister was still standing there. He greeted the Trailors warmly and gave them his blessing. Then he turned away not speaking to Wickersham and walked off.

Wickersham wordlessly helped the family into the wagon, got on his horse and followed them home. The farther they traveled form the church the more Henry and Hattie's shoulders slumped. Adam became agitated not knowing what was wrong and even Abigail became fussy.

When they reached the Trailor house Henry and Hattie unloaded the wagon uncertainly trying not to look at Wickersham.

"Do you have to take him in now?" asked Hattie desperately.

"It's late. Can't you wait until some time tomorrow?"

"I have to take him in, Ma'am," said Wickersham. "There's no way to avoid that. We'll have to leave after breakfast tomorrow."

Late that night Wickersham heard a noise. He sat up to see that Henry was standing over him watching him intently.

"Why don't you sit down, Mr. Trailor?" asked Wickersham.

"What should I do, Mr. Wickersham?" asked Henry. "If anything happens to me what will become of my family? I've done nothing wrong. I hurt nobody. I don't know what happened to Mr. Fisher. What do you want me to do? What should I say?"

"You should cooperate with Mr. Lamborn, the attorney general," said Wickersham, "and tell the truth."

Wickersham hesitated, remembered his private instructions and then continued, "There's no hope for you otherwise and your family will lose you."

Henry rocked back and forth moaning softly.

"I can't leave my family unprotected," said Henry. "Tell me what you want me to say."

Wickersham felt temptation rising in his mind. It would be so easy to instruct this desperate man what to say. He would probably repeat it word for word. The sheriff and the attorney general would be so pleased to get a confession that they would not inquire too deeply into how it was obtained. Even if Henry recanted later, Wickersham could testify about what Henry had said. He formed the words in his mind. He also remembered his conversation with Jim Maxey. There was a man to admire thought Wickersham.

He was not easy to warm up to but once he was your friend. He would be your friend forever.

"Just, just tell the truth," said Wickersham suddenly. "Tell it in your words as it happened. That's the best you can do. That's the best any man can do. Being honest. Telling the truth. Then you can live with what you've done; whatever it is."

"You keep acting like I've done something," said Henry. "I haven't done anything."

"Then that's what you need to say," said Wickersham. "Mr. Trailor, there are no magic "Open Sesame" words that will get you out of this. You've got to ride out the storm as it happens, and until it's over. Now, it's very late and it's your last chance for some time to comfort your wife. Why don't you go back to her and hold her."

After that, Wickersham slept with an untroubled conscience. The next morning Henry appeared pale and drawn. His eyes were red. His face was nicked where he had cut himself having. Hattie seemed in little better shape. She moved about the house with a trembling lip and shaking hands. But she did not cry. She made breakfast for the men and fixed them something to eat on the way.

Wickersham allowed the couple a time to themselves out of earshot.

"Henry Trailor," said Hattie, "you promise me that you will do anything you have to do to come back to me and your family. Whatever it takes, you do it. Promise me."

"All right. I promise."

The men saddled their horses and rode off toward Springfield. Henry looked back often and waved. Even after the figures dwindled to specks and disappeared he looked back wondering if he would ever see his family again.

"You slept pretty easy in the house of a man supposed to be a killer,," said Henry to Wickersham.

"I didn't expect you to be any trouble," said Wickersham. "It would be a pretty cold killer who'd kill a man in the same house his wife and children were asleep in."

"I'm supposed to be a cold killer," said Henry.

They rode in silence for some time.

"The people in my church. They didn't seem to think I was the killer I'm made out to be. Maybe I'll get men like that on the jury."

"I don't mean to discourage you but those folks were your neighbors. The jurors will be people who live in Springfield. Not too many know you there. The ones who do, know you from your wilder days. The rest only know what they've been told about you. You better think on getting yourself a lawyer like that Mr. Lincoln."

Henry retreated into a depressed silence for the rest of the trip.

Chapter Fourteen

Monday, June 14, 1841 Springfield, Illinois

When Wickersham and Henry rode into town people stopped what they were doing to stand and watch them ride by. The people stood silently until they passed by. Some people returned to their business but others followed the men down the dusty street until it looked like a fourth of July parade. Taverns emptied as drunken men exited to follow the crowd. Children ran after the horses yelling and whooping like Indians.

Henry looked back at the people following them nervously.

"It seems like most people are declaring a holiday," said Wickersham. "Don't let them worry you. This is the biggest thing to happen in Springfield since they laid the cornerstone to the state capital."

"I thought it might be a lynch mob," said Henry.

"You wouldn't see women and children in a lynch mob," said Wickersham. "People are in too good a mood for that kind of thing. This is more like the way people act when the circus coming to town."

They rode to the jail.

"I'll leave you here," said Wickersham.

"You'll be back won't you?" asked Henry.

"Sure I will. I have some things to attend to and I'll be back to see you tonight."

"You promise?" asked Henry.

"You have my word on it," said Wickersham.

Henry entered the jail meekly and allowed himself to be locked into a cell without protest.

The jailer was a fragile-looking old man with a fringe of white hair around his head and watery blue eyes known as "Pap" Douglas.

"Where are the sheriff and the attorney general?" Wickersham asked Douglas.

"They're with the mayor at Keys' tavern," answered Douglas. "They said you was to go down there as soon as you got in."

Wickersham made his way to the tavern.

"Hail the man of the hour," announced the mayor, Alvan Martin, spotting Wickersham. "We heard about your parade down main street. I guess today you could be elected to my job or to the job of anybody here."

Manasseh Porter and Ignatius Langford looked away from the map on the wall and nodded. Wickersham noticed that the map on the wall showed investigations in the area north and west of Springfield.

"Thank you," said Wickersham. "I'll just keep my own job if it's all the same with you."

"Alonzo, what happened with Henry Trailor?" asked Caleb Young, the sheriff.

Wickersham looked around the tavern at the men coming and going. Several men were standing or sitting close by studiously pretending not to be listening. Dennis Kelly had a half-empty bottle of whiskey on the table in front of him. He seemed determined to see how quickly he could empty the rest of the bottle.

"Do you want me to tell you here?" asked Wickersham. "Or should I tell you privately?"

"Alonzo, you've been out of town so you don't know but the men in the tavern here have been assisting us in the investigation since the beginning. Anything you have to say can be said in front of them," said Lamborn.

"These men are fine upstanding citizens," said Martin. "It would be cruelty itself to exclude them from this discussion."

Wickersham looked at sheriff Young for direction. He avoided eye contact and said nothing.

"Sheriff, did you want me to talk to you here?"

The sheriff nodded.

"Very well," said Wickersham. "I arrested Henry Tailor and brought him back. He's in the jail right now."

"Did he give you any trouble? Young asked.

"Nary a bit," answered Wickersham.

"Good man," said Young.

"What's his mood?" asked Martin.

"He's terrified," answered Wickersham. "He didn't sleep much last night. He hasn't eaten much today. He's so frightened that he can't even think straight."

"What specifically is he terrified of?" asked Lamborn.

"He's terrified he will hang," said Wickersham. "He's afraid he will never see his family again. He's afraid his wife will become a widow and his children will lose their father. He's scared because doesn't know what to say about Mr. Fisher disappearing."

"So he might be amenable to a little direction on the matter," said Lamborn.

"He might," answered Wickersham. "He asked me what he should say."

"And just what did you tell him when he asked that?" asked Martin.

"I told him to tell the truth, of course," said Wickersham. "What would you have me say to the man?"

"Oh, exactly what you told him," said Martin quickly. "I wouldn't have it any other way."

Lamborn glared at Martin who looked away.

"Did Henry Trailor say anything about killing Mr. Fisher?" asked Lamborn.

"No sir."

"Did he say anything about his brothers killing Mr. Fisher?" asked Lamborn.

"No sir."

"Did he indicate in any way that he knew where the body might be found?" asked Lamborn.

"No sir."

"Did he change his story and give inconsistent details?" asked Lamborn.

"No sir."

"Did he claim he did not kill Mr. Fisher?" asked Lamborn.

"Yes sir," answered Wickersham.

Lamborn looked around at the men in the tavern. He gave Wickersham a hard look. Wickersham looked back at him calmly without speaking.

"Was Mr. Trailor able to explain in detail what happened to Mr. Fisher?" asked Lamborn.

"He was not," answered Wickersham.

"Was he able to explain what happened to Mr. Fisher in a general way?"

"He was not."

"Did he tell you how it was that the man disappeared?"

"He did not."

"Did he explain how his brother came to possess several gold pieces?"

"No sir."

"Did he explain why people in William Trailors community wrote us a letter stating that William was bragging he inherited money from Mr. Fisher?" asked Lamborn.

"No sir," answered Wickersham.

"So according to Henry Trailor, Mr. Fisher up and vanished into thin air," said Lamborn. "He offers no reasonable explanation as to Mr. Fisher's whereabouts. He offers no explanation as to his brother's sudden wealth. He offers no reason that William's neighbor think he is a murderer."

"Alonzo, you did well," said Young. "Why don't you take the rest of the day off."

"Thank you, sir," said Wickersham. He nodded to the men and left the tavern.

The onlookers, thinking the show was over when back to their own business.

"I thought you talked to Alonzo," said Martin. "I thought he understood what we wanted him to do."

"I thought he did too," said Lamborn. "We surely could have used an overheard confession of some sort. Even if he recanted later Henry Trailor would have had a difficult time explaining that away. Mr. Wickersham would have been a heroic young witness."

"He just did his job," said Young. "Let him be."

"That little speech I made may work in a tavern," said Lamborn. "In a court of law where there is a lawyer defending them we're going to need a lot more than we have."

Lamborn looked at the map on the wall. "We need to concentrate all our efforts to the north and to the west of town. Would you coordinate that, Sheriff Young? The mayor and I need to pay a visit to the newest resident of the jail. Mr. Trailor is tired, hungry, and so frightened that he can not think clearly."

Lamborn clapped Martin on the back.

120

"Mr. Mayor, you're about to become the best friend poor Mr. Henry Trailor ever had. I, on the other hand, am about to become his worst nightmare."

Wickersham stopped by the jail briefly and spoke to Henry Trailor who seemed pathetically glad to see him. When Pap Douglas wandered over to listen Wickersham joked to Henry, "Don't try to pull anything on this old coot. He might look like he's about to dry up completely and blow away but he's been a jailer for longer than I've been alive. He's seen every trick in the book."

"And several that didn't pass the publisher," boasted Douglas.

"He's older than the hills, but can fight dirtier than any other man in town," said Wickersham.

Then Wickersham went over to the law offices of Logan and Lincoln. Logan said that Lincoln was out of town trying cases on the judicial circuit. Logan promised to tell Lincoln, when he returned from the circuit, that Henry Trailor was in jail and needed a lawyer. While Wickersham headed home, Lamborn and Martin headed toward the jail.

Henry sat on the bunk in his cell with his arms wrapped around his knees and his eyes closed. He looked up startled when the door to the cell clanged open. Lamborn and Martin entered the cell together. Lamborn stood and glowered silently at Henry.

Martin stuck out his hand toward Henry.

"I'm Alvan Martin, the mayor of Springfield," said Martin. "This is Josiah Lamborn, the attorney general for the state of Illinois."

Henry shook hands with Martin automatically. Lamborn stood with his arms crossed.

"Stand up!" demanded Lamborn abruptly.

Henry nearly leapt to his feet. Lamborn looked him up and down.

"How much do you weigh?" asked Lamborn.

"Well, I don't know exactly."

Lamborn shook his head as if he were disgusted. "You don't weigh enough to make much difference."

"I don't understand," said Henry.

"The rope," said Lamborn. "When we hang a really heavy man we have to use a thicker rope. Sometimes a man's head will pop right off and that makes a mess. When we hang you it'll only take the usual rope."

Henry's mouth dropped open.

"There's no reason to go talking to the man like that," insisted Martin.

"Look," said Henry, "I didn't do anything wrong. You've got to believe me."

"Yeah, sure," said Lamborn. "All the men I hang say that. You're all saints. You're all innocent. At least you are to hear you talk."

"Maybe he didn't do anything wrong," said Martin.

"Maybe Mr. Fisher grew wings and flew away," said Lamborn.

"Maybe his brother, William, discovered where Captain Kidd buried his treasure and that's where he got all those gold pieces."

"You don't have to be like that, Mr. attorney general," said Martin.

"Mr. Trailor, you and your brothers chose the wrong town to murder somebody in," said Lamborn. "You brought your evil ways to the place I live in. I don't like messes left right on my doorstep. When I clean them up I don't allow even a drop of mess to remain."

"Now, now," said Martin, "maybe Mr. Trailor can help you clean up the mess."

"I don't see how," said Lamborn. "I've had the men of this town tilt her on her ear to see what falls out and I've just about got the whole thing reckoned."

Henry opened his mouth at last and the two men lean forward expectantly.

"I don't know what you're talking about." said Henry in a shaky voice. "My brothers and I did nothing wrong. We didn't kill Mr. Fisher or anybody else."

"There, you see," said Lamborn, "I knew he'd be useless. I don't need him either."

"Give him a chance," said Martin.

"You talk to him," said Lamborn. "I'm too disgusted to bother."

Lamborn banged on the door. Douglas showed up almost instantly and let Lamborn out. Lamborn walked around the corner of the cell and stopped. Out of Henry's sight he listened intently.

"You shouldn't have done that," said Martin. "You made him angry. You'd do better to cooperate."

"But I don't know anything," insisted Henry.

"Well friend," said Martin, "you can keep up that posture if you choose. Like the man said, it's your neck."

Martin knocked on the door until Douglas let him out. Lamborn motioned to both men to be quiet. They went through the door into the outer room.

"Very well done," said Lamborn to Martin. "Get some dinner and a rest and then come back here to talk to him again. Douglas, look in on him from time to time. If he gets too comfortable or starts to fall asleep start a conversation with him. Talk about hangings you've seen or something like that to keep his attention on his peril. The mayor and I will take shifts of talking with him. I'll arrange for some relief for you during the night. If he asks for food, give him some. But make it poor quality food and not too much of it. I want him tired and hungry. Is that clear?"

Martin and Douglas nodded. Douglas went back to keep an eye on the prisoner. Throughout the afternoon Lamborn and Martin took turns going at Henry. Arch Trailor came to the jail and tried to see Henry. Acting according to instructions, Douglas turned him away and told him not to return.

"We are working him like a pierce of raw iron," said Lamborn at one point. "You thrust him into the fire to soften him up and then I hammer him on the anvil to shape him."

Lamborn and Martin took turns to make certain that each man was fresh while Henry became more and more worn out. They continued late into the night with Henry continuing to protest his innocence. The interrogation finally stopped long enough to allow Henry to catch a few hours of fitful sleep.

Monday, June 14, 1841 Springfield, Illinois

Sheriff Young sent Wickersham out of town to insure that a family moved off a farm that had been repossessed. He gave Wickersham instructions to help the family move its belongings and told him take as much time as he needed. The representative of the bank and the farmer argued over which animals the bank owned and which would accompany the farmer. Wickersham had to mediate the disputes. The family moved in with relatives who lived nearby but it took the entire day to load the wagons, move at the speed of the slowest animals and to unload at the other end of the journey. The family insisted on feeding Wickersham in thanks for his efforts. Wickersham was afraid if he did not stay for a meal, the proud family would think he was refusing the meal out of pity, so he stayed to eat with them. He was not able to return until that night. It did not occur to Wickersham to visit Henry that night.

Meanwhile, in Springfield, Young coordinated the efforts of Porter and Langford in continuing the search northwest of town. Lamborn and Martin continued to work on Henry in the jail. Lamborn found a man who could relieve Douglas in the jail. Part of the reason the man was hired was that he was learning to play the fiddle. His squeaks and squawks penetrated all corners of the building. By the evening Henry could doze off even when the fiddle was being played. Arch Trailor appealed to the sheriff who told him that the attorney general would not allow anyone to see Henry.

Monday, June 14, 1841 Danville, Illinois

Abraham Lincoln set the papers he had been reading down slowly and stared at the young man in front of him with anger in his eyes. "It is clear to me that the man who signed these papers was a fool. He had the discredit of leaving his widow and his children bereft not only of his care and protection but also likely bereft of the only money they have in the world.

"Yes, we can doubtless gain your case for you. We can set a whole neighborhood at loggerheads. We can distress a widowed mother and her six fatherless children, and thereby get for you six hundred dollars to which you seem to have legal claim but which rightfully belongs, it seems to me, as much to the woman and her children as it does to you. You must remember that some things legally right are no morally right. We shall not take your case, but we will give you a little advice for which we will charge you nothing. You seem to be a sprightly energetic man; we would advise you to try your hand at making six hundred dollars in some other way."

Chapter Fifteen

Tuesday Morning, June 15, 1841 Springfield, Illinois

Sheriff Young sent Wickersham out of town carrying legal documents for delivery to sheriffs in two distant towns. He told Wickersham to wait for a reply from each sheriff which he was to bring back to Springfield. He told Wickersham to plan to spend at least two nights out of town.

Meanwhile in Springfield, the search of the area northwest of town continued. The interrogation of Henry Trailor continued and he continued to deny any knowledge about what happened to Mr. Fisher. Arch asked the mayor and the attorney general if he could see Henry. Both men turned him down.

Dennis Kelly, the whiskey seller, showed up at a house Arch was repairing with G.W. G.W. was a black man with a strong physique and skin the color of rich earth. Arch and G.W. were hanging a door when Kelly suddenly appeared like a snake flashing out of its hole. Kelly was roaring drunk instead of his usual steady level of intoxication. He swayed unsteadily on his feet.

"Well, you succeeded this time," said Kelly. "I'm out of Myers boarding house now and I'm staying at Keys' tavern. I like it better there. I'm closer to the whiskey." Kelly doubled over laughing at what he evidently thought was a great joke.

"I don't know what you're talking about," said Arch. "I don't decide who boards there, Mrs. Myers does."

"Hide behind a woman," said Kelly. "That's good. That's good. It won't help you in the long run but it's a good excuse all the same. I just came to tell you that I'm going to dance a jig at your hanging. I'll sell as lot of whiskey at your wake. Even a rattlesnake gives a warning rattle before he strikes and I'm giving my tail a shake. If you're a smart man you'll get on your horse and head out of town without ever looking back."

Again Kelly bent over laughing.

"You don't believe me," said Kelly. "Your type never does. It's amazing. Do me one favor, then. Just remember to look for me from the scaffold. I'll be the one waving a flag and yelling the loudest."

Arch and G.W. stopped working to regard the drunken man. Kelly looked at G.W. and bowed.

"Don't think I've forgotten you either," said Kelly. "Back home we know how to deal with Darkies that put on airs. You may be a free man here but sleep lightly. A healthy buck like you would bring a good price in the deep south." Kelly turned on his heel and walked away.

"What a drunk," said Arch. "He's full of wind and piss."

"Don't take him too lightly," said G.W. "A man like that runs on hate. Hate is a powerful force."

"I didn't do anything to him," said Arch. "He doesn't have any reason to hate me."

"That doesn't matter," said G.W. "The hate comes from inside that man. Lots of people hate other people without reasons. It doesn't make them any less dangerous. As much as he drinks, hate probably keeps him alive. Without hate that man would probably just lay down and die."

Tuesday Morning, June 15, 1841 Warren County, Illinois

Jim Maxey arrived at William Trailor's farm in the middle of the morning. He sat tiredly in his saddle and surveyed the area. The fields were weeded and neatly plowed. The crops were green and growing. The buildings were freshly painted and well maintained. The animals looked healthy.

Maxey automatically examined the lay of the land mentally checking for spots from which an ambush could occur and places where a man could be hiding out. The land had rich black earth and a gently rolling contour with good drainage. Maxey thought to himself, my father would have thought he had died and gone to heaven if he ever had a farm like this.

He urged his horse on toward distant figures in one of the fields. Maxey knew that the news of his errand had gone rushing ahead of him like a summer thunder storm crossing the prairie. William Trailor knew he was coming. His family knew he was coming. By this time they knew there was only one man to take William back to face trial. They could have a reception ready.

Maxey checked to make sure he did not make a silhouette against the sky as he rode toward the figures. He had no intention of being an easy target for an unseen gunman. As he neared the figures he saw that one figure was directing a team of heavy workhorses harnessed to a large partially removed stump. Four figures with long poles, shovels and axes seemed to be trying to force the stump out of the ground.

They were so intent on their work that the figures did not seem to notice Maxey's approach until he was nearly on top of them.

Maxey purposefully rode out of the sun so the figures had to squint to see him.

"Good Morning," called Maxey.

The sweaty men standing by the partially removed stump looked up and stopped working. Maxey easily picked out William Trailor from the description he had been given. Two younger men who were obviously brothers were clearly William's sons. The other man was closer in age to William. He was stout as a barrel with a red face and gray hair. He could have been a hired hand except that, dirty as he was, he had an air of calm competence about him. Maxey concluded he was probably a neighbor and a farm owner or a family friend. He noted that none of the men had a weapon although, of course, their tools could be used against him. He looked at the figure driving the horses and stopped short in surprise.

That figure was a woman. She was dressed in rough work clothes. Wisps of her hair, escaped from her sun hat, and looked like coppery gold. Sweat trickled down her muddy, freckled cheek tracing her cheekbone. She shielded her light blue eyes from the sun with a dirty hand. Maxey thought he had never seen a more beautiful woman in his life.

"Who are you?" she asked sharply.

Maxey heard the sound of harps in her voice.

"I'm Jim Maxey, deputy from Springfield," said Maxey.

"You've come to take my father away for trial," she accused.

"Yes, miss. I have," Maxey answered. He prayed that she was a miss and not someone's wife. No one corrected him.

"Mr. Maxey, " don't suppose it will make any difference when I tell you that I am innocent," said William

130

"No sir," said Maxey. He forced himself to look away from the woman and at William. "I'm sorry but it does not. I'm here to take you back to Springfield for trial on the charge of murdering Mr. Fisher. The jury will decide your guilt or innocence, I'm also charged to return with the postmaster and any other witnesses I can find."

"You'll want to take me then," said the red-faced man. "I'm George Digby. William here bought my farm with gold and silver coins. They are supposed to be from Mr. Fisher's treasure, or so I've heard."

"I'm forgetting my manners," said William. "These are my sons, Enoch and Daniel. You've already spoken to my daughter, Cassandra."

Reluctantly, they acknowledged Maxey.

"I heard you were coming," said William. "I had hoped to get this stump out of the ground before I had to leave."

"It looks like you're nearly there," said Maxey. "Why don't you give it another try?"

"I suppose you'll kindly round up your witnesses why we sweat in the sun," snapped Cassandra.

"I could do that," said Maxey. "But with the way any new thing attracts attention in the country I expect the witnesses have already heard that I am here and are already headed here themselves. They've heard about my coming here just like you did. With your permission I'll give you a hand at this instead."

Maxey got off his horse and rolled up his sleeves. For the next half-hour the men dug and pried at the stump while Cassandra guided the horses. She chided the horses sharply and they strained with effort. Finally, with an uneven series of jerky movements the stubborn ground finally yielded the stump.

"Thank you for your help, Mr. Maxey," said William. "We weren't getting anywhere without you."

"Nonsense," said Maxey. "You had it loosened up before I even arrived. You did most of the work. I just got here in time for the celebration."

The men cleaned up at the house with water from the well. Maxey quietly asked the two young men to step far enough away so they would not be overheard. Then he spoke with Enoch and Daniel.

"I know that the two of you have thought about trying to stop me from bringing your father in," said Maxey. "If it were my father, that's what I'd be thinking of. I recommend against it. Your family has trouble enough already. Even if you succeeded, others would follow me searching for him. I can't see you and your father living on the run for the rest of your lives."

"Father made us promise to let you have him," said Enoch.

"It is not a promise that sits us well," said Daniel.

"I understand that and respect it," said Maxey. "Sometimes it is harder to do what you know to be right than it would be to do what you know to be wrong."

"Father thinks God will protest him," said Daniel. "I wish I could be as easy in my mind as he is."

Waiting for Maxey at the house were Alexander Baldwin, postmaster of the county and Mildred Goodwin, a local widow.

Maxey decided to speak to the widow first. She was waiting in the dining room. When Maxey entered he found her closely inspecting the wallpaper as if she were considering buying the place.

"You wanted to speak to me, Ma'am?" asked Maxey.

"If you are the deputy from Springfield I do," said Mildred.

"I am. What can I do for you?"

"I want you to take me to Springfield with you so I can testify at William Trailor's trial."

"What is it, Ma'am, that you can testify to?"

"Many things," said Mildred, "I can tell you that there is not much about this family that has escaped my notice. Although they have many people fooled, they have not pulled the wool over my eyes."

"Yes, Ma'am, but what you know may not bear on the trial. What, if anything, do you know about the possibility that William Trailor murdered Mr. Fisher?"

"I can tell you that Mr. Trailor is a man who could do anything. He makes promises he does not keep. He encourages others into folly so he can laugh at them. He is an evil, evil man."

"And you know that how?" asked Maxey.

"You must not repeat this," said Mildred.

"You must understand that what you tell me could be something you are required to say under oath in court."

"Under oath in court." repeated Mildred. She shuddered dramatically but there was a smile on her lips. "It is my duty. I suppose. After William's dear wife, Sarah, died, he indicated a wish

133

to...That is he suggested as two people left alone in the world we could seek in each other...I hope the implication is clear to you."

"I think I understand," said Maxey gravely. "But this, uh, understanding, I take it did not come to pass."

"Exactly," said Mildred. "He made the implied promise and then he did not follow through."

"I see," said Maxey. "I don't wish to be... indelicate, but you... it was an implied promise. It, then, was not..."

"Stated in so many words. No," said Mildred. "Still, his intentions were made entirely clear."

"I do not doubt that for a minute, Ma'am. And then?"

"Nothing," said Mildred. "Simply nothing happened. I was there. I was waiting. The man did nothing. Can you believe it?"

"Remarkable," said Maxey. After a minute he continued. "Unfortunately because the understanding was, as you put it, not stated in so many words it would be difficult for a court to understand."

"I could also testify about that daughter of his, Cassandra."

"The one who lives here?" asked Maxey.

"The very same," said Mildred. "Would you believe she did nearly the same thing with my son? She encouraged him to think she cared for him. Then, when he spoke to her father, he told my boy that Cassandra liked him as a friend, but she did not think of him as a potential husband. I could testify to that too."

Mildred leaned close to Maxey and continued in a confidential tone of voice. "I have my suspicions about her. I believe that if she was willing to turn down a fine boy like my Ephraim she must have another man in mind."

Maxey felt his pulse speed up. "Have you found out who it is?"

"Well, not yet," admitted Mildred. "She's free and easy around all the young men. She'd probably call it friendly. But she doesn't seem to have one particular beau. I've wondered if she is interested in a man who already belongs to another woman. Someday I'll find out. You just wait."

Maxey felt embarrassed and ashamed that he had encouraged this woman's gossip. A part of him was relieved to learn that she had no intended fiancée.

"Again," said Maxey, "You wouldn't be allowed to testify about this. You have suspicions but in a court of law we need facts."

"I heard the minister denounce William in church," said Mildred. "I flatter myself that I influenced the man to think along those lines."

"I do believe you," said William. "You are an unusually persuasive woman."

"Why, thank you, kindly sir," said Mildred. She smiled.

"Would it be possible for the minister himself to testify?" asked Maxey.

"I'm afraid not," said Mildred. "He now denies that he was even denouncing William. He spouts some nonsense about not judging others and thinking ill of our neighbors."

"I'm sure you haven't changed your ideas," said Maxey.

"Oh no. What I fasten onto I hold fast."

"I'm afraid if the minister testifies that he was not denouncing William that would be considered direct testimony. What you say would be indirect. Besides, William is being accused of murder not of being denounced in church."

"I see," said Mildred.

"I am afraid that you don't have anything to testify about in court," said Maxey. "However, if it is any consolation, you have helped me greatly to understand how things came to be as they are."

"Really?" asked Mildred.

"Most assuredly," answered Maxey.

Mildred felt disappointed that she was not going to testify but she was gratified that the deputy had listened to her so intently. She thought she had done as much as anyone could and fulfilled her Christian duties. She smiled sympathetically at Cassandra as she left the room. Then she allowed Ephraim to drive her home. With satisfaction she thought that Cassandra would see how attentive Ephraim was to his mother and regret that she let him slip from her grasp.

After Mildred left Cassandra tapped on the door to the dining room. When she heard, "Come in." She entered. She found Maxey sitting pensively with his chin in one hand.

"If I may ask," said Cassandra. "What did you learn from our famous widow?"

"I learned that she influenced the minister in his sermon. He now says he did not denounce your father from the pulpit."

"Actually, Reverend Weaver started to denounce him, but he was overcome by his good sense and his conscience."

"Those are things to admire in a minister or any other man. I wonder what else in the letter the postmaster sent to Springfield she influenced," said Maxey. "She is one evil woman."

"When she's in the house, I've seen her examine the curtains, and check out the china. She acts like she's the tax assessor."

"She could probably tell your financial value more accurately than the tax man," said Maxey.

"I used to think she had designs on my father, but I've decided that what she's really interested in is the farm."

"She wanted to testify at the trail," said Maxey. "I told her that there was nothing she could testify to."

Cassandra exhaled. "Thank you very much. I was afraid she would persuade you to take her along. She can be quite persuasive in her suspicions in front of people who don't know her. She could really perform for a jury."

"I'll bet your right," said Maxey.

"Strangely enough, her son is a thoroughly good man. At one time I thought I might be interested in him, but I could not imagine having her as a mother-in-law."

"She mentioned something about that, after talking about how your father gave her certain expectations he never followed up on. She implied that the apple doesn't fall far from the tree."

"Really?" asked Cassandra. "Sometimes my friends and I call her the "blackening widow."

Maxey laughed. "I like that. I'll bet she doesn't allow any reputation to escape her web unblemished."

"Did she tell you that I toy with men's affections?" asked Cassandra.

"I believe something like that came up in the conversation," said Maxey.

"Did she also tell you that, when I find a man I can admire as much as my father, I plan to be as steady as a rock with him?" asked Cassandra.

"No, I don't think she did," said Maxey. He looked into Cassandra's eyes and felt his heart pounding.

"Hello, are you ready for me?" said a voice from the doorway.

Cassandra left the room quickly without saying a word. A tall heavy man with a bald head and a grizzled beard came into the room.

"I'm Alexander Baldwin, postmaster for the county," said the man. "I heard you were coming and I came here to see if you wanted to talk to me."

Maxey forced his thoughts away from Cassandra. He noticed the obvious intelligence in the man's gray eyes.

"Thank you, Mr. Baldwin." Maxey. "You're just the man I want to talk to."

"I know you just talked to our local predatory widow," said Baldwin. "If you take what she says and turn it on its head you'll be just about right. I knew Goodwin before he married that woman and he was a good man. She just ate him up inside over the years until he was a hollowed out shell that walked and talked like a man. It was a shame. She's commenced to try the same with her son but he's made of tougher stuff than his sire was. He's a little hen pecked but still a real man."

"You sound a little sore about her," said Maxey.

"I am," acknowledged Baldwin. "She skinned me good with that letter she got me to write. What troubles me most is that I should have known better but I wrote it anyway. I'll tell you if I wrote it today it would sound a far shot different."

"How's that?" asked Maxey.

"That minister stuff is plumb wrong," said Baldwin. "Also, I ain't found the man who heard in person that Mr. Trailor claimed he inherited money from Mr. Fisher. It's always somebody heard from somebody else who likely heard from another about it. I even tracked down the old biddies that Widow Goodwin claimed to have heard it from. They didn't hear it direct either."

"Will you testify to that in court?" asked Maxey.

"I sure will," said Baldwin. "I never did intend to get Mr. Trailor in trouble. I don't even know the man except to say 'Hello' to. I was just puzzled as to what happened to Mr. Fisher."

"That puzzles us all," said Maxey."

Tuesday Afternoon, June 15, 1841 Springfield, Illinois

Alonzo Wickersham felt tired to the bone as he rose wearily through the streets of Springfield. The sheriff had sent him on errands from one end of the county to the other without respite. Wickersham had begun to think that the sheriff was acting without good reasons because some of the tasks did not require a sworn deputy.

The main thing on Wickersham's mind was getting to bed until he noticed the jail in the distance. His conscience reminded him that he had not seen Henry Trailor since the first day Henry was jailed. Wickersham reminded himself that he had not exactly promised Henry he would look in on him every day. On the other hand, to Henry it would likely seem to be an age since Wickersham had seen him. Henry was sitting in jail alone. Wickersham turned his horse toward the jail. He dismounted with a groan and stretched his back. Then Wickersham entered the jail. Nobody was in the outside room so Wickersham walked through the door to the cells.

Pap Douglas was napping in chair tipped back against a wall. Henry was dozing on the bunk of his cell. Wickersham immediately noticed that Henry looked older than when last seen. Henry was unshaven and his body odor permeated the room. His face seemed lined and his sleep was uneasy.

"Henry," said Wickersham softly.

Henry woke up slowly and seemed groggy.

"Wickersham," he said desperately. "You've been honest with me. Tell me. What do they want? They won't leave me alone. They won't let me sleep. They won't let me eat. When I ask for a lawyer they tell me that an innocent man doesn't need a lawyer. What can I do?"

Henry's voice woke Douglas up.

"You shouldn't be here," said the jailer to Wickersham.

"When I ask them what will happen to my wife and children, they tell me that she's pretty enough and young enough to get

140

another husband. I want to see my children grow up. What do they want me to do? asked Henry.

"You'd better get out of here," said Douglas to Wickersham.

"I told them the truth like you said. They don't want that. What do they want?" asked Henry.

Wickersham backed out of the room and walked across the street. He went immediately to the sheriff's office and walked in.

"Do you know what they're doing to Henry Trailor?" he demanded.

"I haven't been over to the jail," said Caleb Young. "My guess is they're interrogating him."

"Have you seen him?" asked Wickersham.

"No," said the sheriff, "It sounds like you have. Listen, deputy, I know sometimes it's not an easy thing to see a man undergoing interrogation. Let me ask you. Was he bruised?"

"No."

"Was he bleeding?" asked the sheriff.

"No."

"Were his bones broken?" asked the sheriff.

"No."

"Then he wasn't beaten," said the sheriff. "He's got nothing to kick about."

"He's tired and hungry to the point he can not think," said Wickersham.

"If he's innocent, he's got nothing to worry about and neither do you. You're tired and worn to a frazzle. I've been sending you on too many errands with Maxey out of town. Sleep on it. Visit Henry tomorrow and talk to Mr. Lamborn and Mr. Martin. You'll see that I'm right. What does an innocent man have to fear?"

Tuesday, Afternoon June 15, 1841 Warren County, Illinois

Deputy Maxey was impressed that with so many worries Cassandra was still able to provide a complete and well-made dinner for her family and the visitors to her home. She acted with such grace and composure that Maxey was filled with admiration. He could only imagine the strain the arrest of her father and his upcoming trial put upon her. Maxey wondered what she thought about his role in her father's problems and what, if anything, he could do to alleviate them.

"I'm afraid, sir, that we need to start back after this excellent meal is finished," said Maxey to William.

"There's nothing to be afraid of," said William. "Nothing at all. I did nothing wrong and I can stand, without fear, in front of my maker. I can face God's judgment with a clear conscience."

"Unfortunately father, you will be tried by a court of this earth. That's likely to be a different matter. Isn't that so, Mr. Maxey," said Cassandra

"Yes, Miss," said Maxey. "It is. Mr. Trailor you'll need to defend yourself with vigor against this charge. I know the attorney general. He'll attack you with a vengeance. He does not like to lose regardless of the strength of the case."

"I thank you for your concern, sir," said William, "But there's no need to worry. The Lord is my shepherd. I shall not want. I fear no evil."

Maxey looked at Cassandra. She had a worried expression on her face.

"All the same, sir, when we get back to Springfield your first concern should be to find a good attorney."

"Father, I'm coming with you," said Cassandra

"There's no need for that," said William calmly. "I'll be returning when the trial is over. It won't take that long. Besides, who would cook for your brothers when you're gone?"

"It may not be needful for you, father, but it is for me," said Cassandra. "My brothers should learn how to get along without me. I won't be cooking for them forever, you know."

"What if I say that I don't want you to be at my trial?" asked William mildly.

"Then I won't go to your trial," said Cassandra. "I will, however, attend my uncles' trial." Cassandra crossed her arms and stood waiting.

William smiled at her fondly. "Your mother used to stand just like that when she'd made up her mind to the point that she would not be moved." William. "I never won a serious argument with her either. If you're packed and ready by the time we ready to leave you can come with us."

"You know we can't wait long for you to get ready," said Maxey apologetically.

"Oh, I'm packed," said Cassandra.

Seeing the surprised look on Maxey's face, she added. "Just in case, I packed before. I always could have unpacked."

She picked up some dishes and carried them toward the kitchen.

"She's just like her mother," said William proudly.

Daniel and Enoch watched morosely as William drove the wagon off toward Springfield. He was talking with Cassandra and acting as if he did not have a care in the world. Maxey, Digby and Baldwin rode along side the wagon.

Early in the evening they reached Lewistown, a small town in Fulton County. They stopped for the night at Wilburn's tavern. William continued to act unconcerned. He talked to Digby about combining the farms and expected crop yields. He clearly did not expect the trial to be more than a temporary delay in his plans. Maxey could not remember ever escorting a prisoner who showed such a calm demeanor. Baldwin entertained the group and others staying at the tavern with funny stories about people who stayed at his tavern. He and Wilburn, a short, thin but jovial man, competed to see who could tell the more outrageous tale while keeping the telling appropriate for Cassandra to overhear.

As time passed the night became black. Maxey was gathering his wits and trying to think about what he could say to Cassandra when the door to the tavern was flung open and three travel-stained men entered. Two of the men immediately went over to William and greeted him warmly. They were, obviously, old friends of his. The third man was an older man with a grimy, tired, lined face and wire rimmed glasses showing lively brown eyes. He had sparse gray hair and a wiry build. He was wearing well made but muddy clothes.

He approached Maxey directly. "Are you the deputy from Springfield?" he asked.

"Yes, I'm Jim Maxey." Maxey offered his hand and the man shook it.

"My name is Dr. Asa Gilmore." He said. "I've been riding all day. I'm glad I caught up with you before you took Mr. Trailor back to Springfield with you."

"Do you have something you want to say at his trial?" asked Maxey.

"No," said Dr. Gilmore. "You don't understand. There should not be a trial at all. Archibald Fisher is alive and under my care at home."

The tavern fell silent.

"I was out of my home this morning tending to the birth of twins at the Hutchinsons." said Gilmore. "When I returned about eleven Mr. Fisher was there. He could give no clear account of how he came to be there or where he had been. He gave a confused account and it was clear he had no idea himself of what happened to him. About one o'clock, a friend of William Fisher sent me a note that he had been arrested. He asked that I travel to Springfield to testify about Mr. Fisher's past health problems. With these two good neighbors, old friends of William's, I rode here to tell you."

"God be praised," said William. "I told you all there was no need for a fuss."

"Since his accident two or three years ago," said Gilmore, "Mr. Fisher has periods of mental aberration. This is one of the worst ones I've seen. But before this on several occasions, his senses have become disordered and his thinking has been confused."

145

"Wait a minute," said Maxey. "Let me understand this. You say that Mr. Fisher is at your house. He's...confused but alive."

"Exactly," said Gilmore. "So Mr. Trailor can go home. There was no murder."

"That is wonderful intelligence," said Maxey. "I am delighted. However, I can not let Mr. Trailor go home."

"Why not?" asked Gilmore.

"I don't disbelieve you, sir." said Maxey. "However, I cannot release Mr. Trailor on your word alone."

Maxey glanced at Cassandra silently pleading for understanding.

"You can see him at my house," offered Gilmore.

"Unfortunately, sir, I have not met Mr. Fisher personally. Even if I had. Even if I knew him and saw him alive at your house. Mr. Trailor is under arrest and all I could do would be to testify at the trial as to what I had seen. If you accompany us to Springfield, you can testify at the trail yourself."

"There's no way I can persuade you, then, that Mr. Trailor should be released?" asked Gilmore.

"Perhaps he should be, sir, but I believe it is my duty to return him to Springfield. I urge you to accompany us and I sincerely hope that you will. You can bring Mr. Fisher along with you."

"He's in no shape to travel right now," said the doctor.

"Dr. Gilmore, my father faces a trial for his life," said Cassandra. "Isn't there some way you can bring him to Springfield with you so everyone can see that he's still alive?"

"I'd like to, Miss Trailor but Mr. Fisher just arrived at my home. There's no way to tell if he has internal injuries. I cannot be absolutely certain that he will live, although I believe he will. He has survived much worse. If the trial could be postponed for two weeks, or even one week, he might be well enough to travel."

"I'm afraid that's not likely," said Maxey. "The attorney general is not likely to be willing to wait even one extra day. The trial will probably start the day after we arrive. That's why we need your testimony."

"Let me talk to my neighbors."

Gilmore went over to talk with the men who had accompanied him. A lively discussion followed with many glances over at Maxey and head shaking.

"You're becoming our Moses," said Baldwin to Maxey. "You command a trail of Israelites on a lengthy journey to the Promised Land. All we need is a pillar of fire to light the way."

I hope I don't have as many troubles as he did along the way," said Maxey. "I need to get there before sooner than he did."

Cassandra stood up and silent walked out of the room. Maxey noted to himself that she appeared to be trembling. He cursed himself inwardly. For a wild moment he thought about sending William home and returning to Springfield alone. He wondered if Cassandra would be grateful if he voluntarily faced down the town of Springfield alone. Reluctantly he reminded himself that he had a duty to perform. He had defined his life in terms of duty until it became part of his very identity. Duty had taken him from the life of a farmer's son and an extra hand at harvest, to the position of responsibility and respect he now held. Without duty he was just another farmers son scratching out a living from the dust. Duty made him who he had become a man whose word you could take to the bank. Duty, he thought glumly, also made him a man alone facing a lonely existence.

Gilmore concluded the discussion with his friends and returned to Maxey.

"I've heard you are a man whose word can be trusted," said Gilmore. "If you say you need me to come to all the way to Springfield, I will. I've written a note to my wife explaining my absence from home and giving instructions about the patients that I am currently treating. My neighbors will deliver it. After being married to a doctor for as long as she has, my wife knows just about as much medicine as I do. She can handle my patients temporarily. I guess I'm joining this strange parade."

"Thank you very much, doctor," said Maxey.

"I suppose you're right, about the parade, doctor," said Baldwin, who had been listening intently. "If we had an elephant we could rent ourselves out as a traveling circus."

Maxey waited hopefully but Cassandra did not return.

Tuesday, June 15, 1841 Paris, Illinois

"I tell you, Mr. Lincoln, I want to get the law on Jim Adams. It ain't right that he claims his property goes all the way over here." Tom Adams concluded.

Lincoln sat in his rude buggy and thought for a moment.

"Uncle Tommy, you haven't had any fight with Jim, have you?"

"No."

"He's a fair to middling neighbor, isn't he?"

"Only tolerable, Abe."

"He's been a neighbor of yours for a long time, hasn't he?"

"Nigh onto fifteen years."

"Part of the time you get along all right, don't you?"

"I reckon we do, Abe."

"Well, now, Uncle Tommy, you see this swayback nag of mine? He isn't as good a horse as I could find and sometimes I get out of patience with him, but I know his faults. He does fairly well as horses go, and it might take me a long time to get used to some other horse's failings. You and Uncle Jimmy must put up with each other, as I and my horse do with one another."

"Aw, Abe."

"I mean it, Uncle Tommy. If you take Uncle Jimmy to court you could change a tolerable neighbor into an implacable enemy. Win or lose the case. The law is not something to be trifled with. You don't want to set it loose if you have any doubts about your claim of if there is any other way to settle your differences. It is like a force of nature, like a fire. It can be great tool to help to a man but there can also be a great danger of immolation. "

Chapter Sixteen

Wednesday, Morning June 16, 1841 Springfield, Illinois

Dennis Kelly, the whiskey seller, woke up at dawn with his usual hang over. Deprived of whiskey for the night, his body sent shock waves through his mind demanding alcohol to quiet the pain caused by the relative sobriety. Kelly suspiciously checked to see if any of the other men in the room were awake. Several of them would awaken with a similar need. Given the opportunity they would raid his private stash of alcohol driven by demons greater than their humanity.

Kelly carefully reached under the bedclothes to retrieve his flask. It was not there. On the verge of panic he then remembered that he had changed hiding places. Too many heavy drinking men were becoming interested in his bed. He unobtrusively slipped a hand into his boot and was rewarded by the feel of the flask. He eased it out with a trembling hand, opened it and swallowed the contents in a few deep swallows. That would hold the pain at bay for a while. Now he could attend to the pressure from his bladder and bowels.

Kelly listened to the sounds of the men in the room. Some men snored. In the corner a man whimpered in his sleep. Some men snorted. Others belched or farted. With two or three men in each bed the room was cramped. It smelled of tobacco, sweat, and less pleasant human odors.
Kelly lay on his back staring at the ceiling. He thought about the unfairness of the world and the cruelty of people. It seemed to Kelly that there had always been someone standing between him and the rewards of life he so clearly deserved. For all his life riches, honor,

acclaim, the affection of women, all seemed just outside his grasp. There was always someone blocking his path so the rewards he actually deserved always went to someone else. His father had favored his older brother smoothing the way for him while casting stones onto Kelly's path. When he worked for others, there was always a favored one the bosses liked; usually their sons or other kin. How could a man fight that? He could not. Over the years Kelly had learned how to get back at the favored ones by jokes, and by tricks, he had tasted revenge and he found it as good as whiskey.

Kelly thought about Arch Trailor. Obviously the man had schemed to turn the other boarders against him. Kelly's anger flared when he remembered that James and Hart spoke against him calling him liar for no reason. They trusted in their physical strength knowing that one could back up the other. Two against one. What kind of fight would that have been? Kelly congratulated himself on his good judgment in avoiding that trap. Arch had set him up for humiliation in front of his friends. Then James and Hart threw him out of the most comfortable affordable boarding house in the whole town of Springfield forcing him to board at Keys' tavern. The food here was indifferent at best and the level of conversation was less than what Kelly was used to; less that what he was entitled to.

Arch was one of the favored ones. His older brother gave him a gold piece when Arch left home. Kelly's older brother, another favored one, gave Kelly only curses when he left home. His brother drove him away from what, by rights, should be at least half his. All the commotion was due to some misunderstanding caused by his brother's scheming shrew of a wife. She convinced her husband, Kelly's older brother, that Kelly was lusting after her. All the while, she was the one being overly friendly toward Kelly. Kelly resolved that after he settled Arch's hash, he would return to his brother's home to settle accounts there. Kelly smiled as he imagined how he might bring that about pushing aside the thought that he had never had the nerve to follow up on his imagination.

Kelly remembered that the attorney general asked to meet him just after dawn. He wondered vaguely what Lamborn wanted to talk to him about so early in the morning.

Manasseh Porter, hostler at a livery stable, awakened to the noises made by the horses in the stable below his room as they stamped their feet and whinnied to one another in the early morning. He checked the horses and gave them food and water before cleaning himself up and going for his own morning meal. Porter had decided last night that he could give no more than one additional morning to the search of the area northwest of town. In the morning light he could see no reason to change his mind. His "regiment' was down to just over a dozen men, some of whom had nothing better to do. Only two regiments were searching at all since nothing had turned up yet after so many days of searching.

Manasseh Langford, a mason woke up to the smell of breakfast coming from the kitchen of his own small house. He regretted arguing with his wife last night. Stubborn as the stone he worked with, he had to admit that she was right. He had been losing work to other eager builders because he continued to lead a steadily diminishing number of men searching futilely for evidence of the murder of Mr. Fisher. The work his regiment was doing was hard and boring. He really could not blame the men who had pitched in at first only to resume their former activities when they found no reason to continue. Mrs. Langford had objected to his continued involvement with the search. Of course that meant that Langford was obliged to defend himself. Now he had to find a way to assuage his pride and yet he had little interest in wasting more time and losing more business.

"I don't care what you say," called Langford from the bedroom to his wife. "This morning is the last time I'm going to waste my time searching for Mr. Fisher's."

Mrs. Langford, who had been married to Ignatius for years, was wise enough not to reply.

Downstairs at Keys' tavern late in the morning Attorney General, Lamborn drank coffee for his breakfast while Mayor Martin ate an enormous meal. Deputy Wickersham came in and sat at a table close to the two men.

"We had a good run even if we didn't get anything bout the murder out of it," said Martin.

Martin started to compose a speech in his mind thanking the volunteers for their efforts and reminding them how they had helped achieve justice by proving the innocence of Henry Trailor.

"Henry's fragile as an egg shell," said Lamborn. "He's ready to confess."

"Confess to what?" asked Martin. "I agree that he's about ready to sign anything you put in front of him. He would plead guilty to causing the last bank panic or organizing the Boston Tea Party right now, but so what? If there was a murder, how did it happen exactly? When and where and where's the body?"

"All we need is one small piece of the puzzle," said Lamborn. "One more straw for the camel's back."

"Well, we'd better find it quickly," said Martin.

Henry Trailor woke up slowly. His exhausted body fought to stay asleep but his anguished mind came awake almost against his will. Henry clutched a blanket to his chest. He had dreamed he was home again with Hattie and the children. When Henry realized that he was still in jail tears formed in his eyes. The tears rolled down his unshaven cheeks. His shoulders began to heave. Henry started to sob uncontrollably.

Sheriff Caleb Young felt tired even when he first woke up. Wickersham's questions combined with his own doubts about the treatment of Henry Trailor. He had tried to keep himself away from the investigation even to the point of staying away from the jail just across the street. So far he could say he did not know, at least directly, what was going on with Henry. But his picket line was growing thin as the investigation lumbered ahead slowly with no evidence of progress. As time passed, it was starting to be a fair question to ask why he was not involved.

Young decided to visit Keys' tavern and talk with Martin and Lamborn. He found the men pouring over the map and discussing the area northwest of town where Henry and William left town before returning and leaving a second time to go home. Young noticed that Wilkersham was eating his breakfast at a table close to Martin and Lamborn.

"I'm getting concerned about this investigation," said Young. "Deputy Wickersham over there has been asking about how Henry Trailor is doing in the jail and I'm starting to think he's right. Arch Trailor is asking to see his brother and I've got to do something about that. This whole thing seems to be dragging on to no conclusion. When do you think it's time to call it off?"

"You and everybody else today thinks we should stop," grumbled Lamborn. "I want to have the search cover the area between the road past the brewery and the road past the brick yard. You see how it forms an angle there? If the Trailors used either road to move the body we should find something there."

"How long should that take?" asked Young.

"No more than one day more," said Lamborn. "Do you think you can stand to wait one more day?"

Young hesitated. "What if nothing is found there?" he asked. "Will you call an end to all this and turn Mr. Trailor loose?"

"I promise," said Lamborn, "Bit I warn you. I'm feeling lucky today. If you have a chance to bet wager on me."

"Very well," said the sheriff.

As Young walked away, Martin remarked. "You seem awfully sure of yourself. The searchers are talking about giving it up as a bad job starting this afternoon. The sheriff is getting as nervy as a stallion in heat. What do you have up your sleeve?"

Lamborn lifted a shirt sleeve cuff with his finger and peered inside. "It looks like an arm to me."

When Langford and Porter came into the tavern Lamborn pointed out the area on the map he wanted them to cover that morning. Langford and Porter seemed relieved that Lamborn did not object to their plans to stop searching after that day.

After the regiments left, Lamborn turned to Martin and said, "Let's go pay Henry a visit."

In the jail Henry sat listlessly on his bunk. He looked straight ahead but his eyes seemed vacant.

"Henry, let's get on with this so we can get done with it," said Lamborn.

Henry sat motionless.

"You told us that you and William left town heading northwest before you headed home for good to look at Hitchcock's mill. Is that correct?" asked Lamborn.

155

Henry nodded.

"Please answer questions verbally," said Martin.

"Yes."

"At that time you didn't know Mr. Fisher was dead." Lamborn.

"Yes."

"And you didn't kill Mr. Fisher.," said Lamborn.

"No."

"So, you didn't kill Mr. Fisher, and while you were in Springfield you didn't know he had been killed," said Lamborn.

"Yes."

"You didn't kill him," said Lamborn. "Your brothers must have killed him."

"What do you want me to say?" asked Henry.

"Did you kill him?" asked Lamborn.

"No." Henry.

"Did they kill him?" asked Lamborn.

Henry started to cry.

"They killed him didn't they?" asked Lamborn gently.

"If that's what you want me to say," said Henry. "Yes."

"Yes.," said Lamborn. "Just the truth. It is the truth. Say it."

"It is the truth." repeated Henry mechanically. His eyes were dull and looked out of focus.

"You heard that, Mr. Martin," said Lamborn sharply.

"But you didn't know that they killed him," said Lamborn gently to Henry. "Not right then."

"I didn't know." Henry.

"It was not until you left with William that you found out," said Lamborn.

"I found out."

"Arch showed up northwest of town," said Lamborn. "He and William left you to watch while they took the body."

"They took the body.," said Henry.

"Maybe they put it in the millpond or Spring creek." said Lamborn.

"Mill pond or Spring creek," said Henry by rote.

"Did they back the buggy up to a thicket and put the body in it?" asked Lamborn. "Did they head for the pond and return without the body about half an hour later?"

Henry blinked.

"Yes?" asked Lamborn.

"Yes."

"You heard that, Mr. Martin," said Lamborn. "Henry Trailor said all that without any pressure or duress."

"Yes, he did," said Martin.

157

"Douglas, clean up my friend Mr. Trailor here," said Lamborn. "Get him clean clothes. Give him a shave. Get him a good meal from the hotel. Then let him sleep for as long as he wants. Mr. Martin, I want you to be here when Mr. Trailor wakes up and remind him about what he just said. Keep reminding him that two people heard his confession and that he swore it was the absolute truth."

"What are you going to do?" asked Martin.

"I'm going to tell people about Henry's confession." answered Lamborn.

Lamborn returned to Keys' tavern. He nodded to Kelly who sat at a table red faced and breathing hard. Kelly caught his eye and nodded back once emphatically.

"Listen to me," called out Lamborn in a voice that carried through out the tavern. "Henry Trailor just confessed." The conversations in the tavern ceased abruptly.

"Henry Trailor admitted that when he and William left town the first time," said Lamborn, "that Arch joined them outside of town about where the brick yard road and the brewery road meet to the northwest. He said that Arch and William left him as a guard. They picked up the body of Mr. Fisher from a thicket and carried it away in the direction of the creek and the millpond."

Whispered conversations sprang up all over the tavern.

"Gentlemen," said Lamborn. "Please give me leave to speak. About half an hour to an hour later William and Arch returned saying they put *him* in a safe place. Later William told Henry the night before he knocked Mr. Fisher down with a club and Arch strangled him to death. They hid the body temporarily in the thicket until they could move to a better hiding place."

The noise in the tavern rose to a pervasive mutter.

158

"Gentlemen," said Lamborn, "Please let me continue. It happens that this morning the search groups were sent to the very area on the roads where Arch and William concealed the body. It may be that some evidence of the foul deed still exists at that location."

At that moment a runner came through the tavern door panting.

The man gasped. "Mr. Lamborn, there's some sort of a, I don't know, a tussle ground where the two roads meet. Something the size of a man was drug through the weeds. There are buggy wheels leading away. They get lost in the road wheel marks but at the Hitchcock's millpond there are buggy wheel tracks running down to the edge of the pond and into the pond."

"I told you Arch Trailor was a murder!" shouted Kelly. Shouts of outrage and anger rang out all over the tavern. "He's been lying to us all along. He's been laughing at us behind our backs."

"Gentlemen, gentlemen," shouted Lamborn. "Let's keep out wits about us. Mr. Johnson, you've got the fastest horse here. Ride back to the searchers and tell them to stand guard at the thicket. Let no man stomp through the area. We need to safeguard the areas to make certain any evidence is maintained. Mr. Bell, you run to Dr. Merryman's office and escort him to the scene. Tell him to examine the area closely for any sign of human remains, blood or whatever he can find. Mr. Davis you notify the sheriff. The rest of you take rakes, hoes and poles and search Spring creek and the Hitchcock millpond for the body. Go."

The men stampeded out of the tavern and ran in all directions. Within minutes the town was blazing with talk. The story made the rounds and returned embellished to the point that it was nearly unrecognizable. Old rumors were raked up and improved upon with each telling.

Meanwhile Lamborn stayed in the tavern. He brought a bottle of whiskey from the barkeeper, Edwin Brown, which he presented to Kelly.

"You're not out searching?" Lamborn asked Brown.

"No sir," answered Brown, "Mr. Keys wants me to stay here and serve the men when they come back from the creek and the pond. He said he figures between the swimmers, the divers and the men who fall in from the bank, there will be plenty of men who will want their insides as wet as their outsides."

The men laughed.

"You won't miss the hanging?" asked Kelly.

"We'll probably close for that and near sellout afterward." Brown. "A hanging has to be good for your business too, Mr. Kelly."

"Even better than a prize fight," agreed Kelly.

"It won't hurt your future either, Mr. Lamborn.," said Kelly.

"True. But I'm more concerned that justice is being done. I truly hate the idea that a murderer getting off entirely free. I would do nearly anything to keep that from happening."

Arch Trailor was on the roof of a newly framed room house nailing down shingles with G.W. when an excited man came up to Dutch who was working below.

"Henry Trailor confessed," the man shouted. "He said his brothers killed the man and hid the body in Hitchcock's mill pond north of town."

"That can't be." Dutch said. "I know the men personally."

"Yeah, everybody I tell says that. I don't know the men myself. I'm a salesman just passing through. I reckon they had the whole town buffaloed. They must be slippery as melting ice. People are hotter than blue blazes to think the brothers gulled them. But anyway, I was drinking in Keys tavern when the man came in and told what Henry Trailor said. Mr. Lamborn he was called. Then another man came in and told us they found the place where the Trailors hid the body temporarily. Now they're searching a millpond for the body. I was going to leave town but the big to do is coming. I wouldn't want to miss the rope party." The man hurried off looking for other people to tell his story to. Dutch climbed the ladder and sat down with Arch and G.W.

"I can't believe it." Arch said. "Henry would never say such a thing."

"He's been kept in that jail for a long time now," said G.W. "They wouldn't let you see him. You don't know what they could have done. You don't know what they threatened him with. You don't even know what he said that they could twist into a confession. When they get a man alone and they want something from him bad enough; sooner or later they're going to get it."

"You'd better stay out of sight, Arch," said Dutch. "When the crowd gets liquored up some of them could come looking for you."

"They're my friends," said Arch.

"Not all of them," objected G.W.

"They won't any of them be your friends after they get drunk," said Dutch. "You two finish the roof right quick. Then we have some inside jobs you can work on where you can stay out of sight."

161

"I'm not running away from this."

"Nobody asked you to," said Dutch. "On the other hand, you'd be foolish to stay outside during a hailstorm. If you accidentally bumped into a hornets' nest, you wouldn't stand there explaining how you didn't mean it while you got stung."

"I guess not," admitted Arch.

"I'd like to stay out of sight myself," said G.W. "Once a train starts moving it runs over anything left on the tracks. Lynch mobs are none too particular once they get started. If they see somebody with my skin color, they'd likely string him up just for the fun of it."

At the thicket between the brewery road and the brickyard road Dr. Mark Merryman moved with deliberation and persistence. Dr. Merryman was a vigorous man with strong opinions. He stood over six feet tall with a muscular frame. He was often thought by strangers to be a laborer or a blacksmith. He had black hair, hazel eyes and a dark complexion. Once started on a task, Dr. Merryman ignored time and discomfort until the task was completed. Unlike some doctors in Springfield, he was not dismayed by difficult and unpleasant business. As a result, the attorney general and the sheriff preferred to use his services when legal matters required the use of a physician.

Dr. Merryman started at the tip of the angle formed by the roads and worked his way inch by inch from one side of the thicket to the other. Then he turned in a tight half circle and slowly worked his way back to the side he started from insuring that every bit of the thicket was examined. He moved through weeds and brambles undeterred by the nettles. When he found something of interest he examined it carefully from every angle and mentally plotted the

162

location within the thicket before he touch the item of interest. At times he removed items form the ground and put them in one of a series of envelopes he carried. Dr. Merryman made careful notations on the outside of each envelope and sealed each one with the desired item inside.

The men keeping others from entering the thicket quickly became bored with watching the doctor's slow progress. One produced a deck of cards and soon a low stakes poker game broke out. One of the men charged with protecting the area fell asleep. Another man got bored and wandered off in the direction of town. Dr. Merryman paid special attention to the area where it appeared something (or someone) the size of a man had been dragged through. He nodded to himself in satisfaction when he picked up two items so small as to be almost invisible. He paused only briefly before resuming his slow, steady pace.

At the millpond, in contrast to the slow, organized and purposeful activity at the thicket, the men explored the water enthusiastically but in a disordered, haphazard way. Without direction some men raked or dived into spring creek before and after it ran into the millpond. They made no effort to mark where the search had been so later arriving investigators went over areas examined earlier while long stretches of water went completely unexplored. A number of the searchers showed up in varying states of inebriation. They ignored attempts by others to organize and record the process. Only the regiments of Porter and Langford showed any form of discipline at all.

The noise and commotion attracted Edmund Hitchcock, owner of the mill. Hitchcock was a slight man with red hair and brown eyes. After seeing the drunken men staggering through the mud and falling into the water, he ordered the men to get off his dam and to stay far away from the mill itself. By a combination of inspired blasphemy, a loaded shotgun, and a fiery temper Hitchcock moved the men away from his property. Hitchcock stayed outside by the mill wheel to enforce his edict.

"But Mr. Hitchcock," whined one nearly sober searcher, "evil murder has been done here."

"If any of you touch the wheel or the dam," replied Hitchcock, "another evil murder will happen here."

Finally, after much delay and wasted effort, and at the cost of much frustration, Porter and Langford enrolled the more sober of the searchers into their regiments, divided the tasks and set about to search systematically. Porter started at the junction of the pond and the stream. He divided his men into two teams, one above the millpond and one below the pond. He began to work his way upstream from where the creek entered the pond with half the men. They made certain that the banks, the streambed and any snags observed were thoroughly examined for any sign of tampering. The second team of men started where the steam emerged from the water wheel and worked down stream. Their task was made easier by the fact that the stream was narrower and more rapid after leaving the pond. As a result there were fewer places a body could be concealed.

Langford had the more difficult task of examining the millpond. For some reason the pond seemed to attract the more alcohol-impaired members of the crowd. When they were not obstructing the searchers they managed to fall into the pond, quarrel with each other, or come too close to the mill or the dam for Edmund Hitchcock's taste, thus necessitating one kind of rescue or another. Although the circumference of the pond was not great, the slow moving water was overgrown with weeds both in and out of the water so that it took a long time to cover a small area. The men became sodden and tired which slowed the work even more. Also, there seemed to be an endless supply of troublesome drunks.

Hitchcock very grudgingly and only after a heated exchange with Langford allowed two men under his close supervision to inspect the area adjacent to the mill and the dam.

After several hours, the entire outer edge of the pond was finally covered to Langford's satisfaction. That left the area within the pond. Because of the weeds in the pond and the murky water it was not at all obvious how to proceed.

"We've got to lower the water in the pond somehow," said Langford.

"You've seen all you can see," said Hitchcock. He was sitting on the grass with the shotgun in his lap. "Now get the hell off my property and let me get back to work."

On a good day, with a calm and reasoned approach, or a friendly request for help, Ignatius Langford had been known to change his mind (although rarely.) This was not a good day. The approach was not stated calmly and logically. It was not in the form of a friendly request for assistance.

Langford roared and started for Hitchcock with his hands balled into fists. Hitchcock leapt to his feet and swung the shot gum around to point it at Langford. Langford showed that his command of expletives and curses was close to the level demonstrated by Hitchcock earlier in the day.

"We're going to cut down the dam." He thundered.

"Touch that dam and I'll cot you down," answered Hitchcock.

The two men seemed to be on fire.

"Just what are you trying to hide?" demanded Langford. "Were you in on this with the Trailors? It would explain a lot if they had a confederate in town. Maybe you helped them hide the body."

"I make a living from that dam," shouted Hitchcock. "Go blow up your stone quarry with black powder so you have nothing left to live on and then we'll talk about you breaking my dam."

"Maybe we should save the court some time," said Langford. "We could string you up right here and now."

"I could blow you to kingdom come right now too," said Hitchcock.

"There's too many of us," said Langford. "Shoot me and the rest will hang you anyway." The men began to surround Hitchcock.

"You might kill me but I ain't going alone," said Hitchcock.

"You ain't going anywhere." came a quiet but carrying voice. Deputy Wickersham rode up to the group. "And you, Langford, if you hang anybody the law will hang you. I'd have to explain that to your wife and I wouldn't like that. She'd be mad as a wet hen."

The men laughed and the tension eased.

"The sheriff sent me here to see what kind of foolishness you men were getting yourselves into.]," said Wickersham. "It looks like the sheriff knew what he was talking about."

"You mean there won't be a hanging?" asked one of the drunks.

"Not today, boys." answered Wickersham. "The regiment can stay the rest of you get out of here."

Grumbling and disappointed the men dispersed slowly. Wickersham waited until most had left before dismounting. "What have you two Billy goats gotten into?"

"He threatened to ruin my dam and hang me," said Hitchcock.

"I need to search the pond," answered Langford. "That's where the body most likely is. He knows it and won't let us look. I figure he helped them hide the body. That's why he doesn't want us to search the pond bottom. He was going to blow me up with that shot gun to cover up."

"Nobody's going to hang or get blown up," said Wickersham. "Is that clear?"

The men nodded.

"Hell, I couldn't have shot him, said Hitchcock. "The gun wasn't loaded. I just didn't want the drunks to mess with my water wheel or my dam. That other stuff is just foolishness."

"I didn't know that the gun wasn't loaded," said Langford.

"It's a good thing you didn't. Otherwise you would have ruined my dam and killed me in a snap."

"That's enough." Wickersham.

"We've still got to search the pond," insisted Langford. "The body might be there. We can't allow anybody to get away with murder."

"All of you are interested in justice, then?" asked Wickersham.

The men all concurred.

167

"Very well," said Wickersham. "We'll do this justly. Mr. Hitchcock, you tell these men how to dismantle your dam. You men do it exactly that way. After the water goes down, you can make your search. Then, every single one of you will stay right here and rebuild the dam until it is repaired exactly the way Mr. Hitchcock wants it. Not even one of you will depart until Mr. Hitchcock is satisfied in every particular. Is that agreed?"

After some shuffling of feet and muttering the men agreed. With the promise of help to repair the dam, Hitchcock had the men open a large hole in the dam close to the water wheel so the pond would drain quickly and so that he would be able to use the mill again as quickly as possible.

Chapter Seventeen

Wednesday, Afternoon June 16, 1841 Springfield, Illinois

When Henry Trailor awoke he felt like a new man. His body was clean. He had been shaved. His hair had been trimmed. He was no longer hungry.

"So you're back with us now," said Martin in a friendly voice.

"I, I feel much better now," said Henry.

"Confession will do that for a man," said Martin. "I can't imagine why it took you so long to tell us."

"Me neither. What is it that I confessed to?"

Martin laughed. "That's a good one, Henry. I can call you Henry can't I? Mr. Trailor sounds so formal after all we've been through together. You told us that you didn't kill Mr. Fisher."

"Of course not."

"At first you didn't even know about the murder."

"If something happened to him, I didn't know about it," Henry said in a quavering voice.

"Then the first time you and William left town, out by where the brewery road and the brickyard road meet, William told you," said Martin. "He said that he and Arch had killed Mr. Fisher. They hid his body in a thicket. They left you to guard and drove off with his body. Then they returned without the body."

169

"Where did they put him?" asked Henry.

"You don't know for sure," said Martin. "Maybe in the creek or the millpond."

"How did they kill him?" asked Henry.

"William hit him over the head with a club. Then Arch strangled him."

"When did they kill him?" asked Henry.

"You don't know exactly," answered Martin, "most likely the day when he disappeared."

"Why did they kill him?" asked Henry.

"For the gold he had. He didn't have as much as they thought but they took what he had."

"Oh my. I told you all that?"

"Oh, yes," said Martin. "You told Mr. Lamborn, the attorney general, and me. We both heard it. You told us everything on your own, voluntarily, without being under any pressure at all. You love your brothers but your conscience wouldn't let you keep covering up for them."

"I felt tired, hungry, confused, angry," said Henry.

"Yes," said Martin. "You felt terrible pangs of guilt from your conscience. In the end you had to tell us the truth. Now you feel much better."

"I do feel better," said Henry uncertainly.

"Of course you do. You wouldn't want to feel so bad again would you?"

"No."

"Then all you have to do is to keep telling us the truth like you're doing right now," said Martin. "You would never lie and say terrible things like about your brothers would you?"

"No." Henry answered slowly.

"So what you told us has to be the truth," said Martin. "There's no doubt about it at all. You were loyal to your brothers for as long as possible but you couldn't let their terrible crime go unpunished."

"Oh. Can I go back to sleep now?" asked Henry.

"Of course," said Martin, "if you're hungry when you wake up again, let me know. If you need another blanket, tell me. If you need anything, Mr. Lamborn or Pap Douglas or I will be here all the time. Don't worry about a thing."

Henry went back to the bed. "I told you all those things?"

"Yes, of course," said Martin. "How else would we know all about it? Go back to sleep now. You need the rest."

Arch Trailor and G.W. Turner were putting kitchen cabinets into a newly built house when Dutch came in looking very somber.

"They found a place close to the Hitchcock mill that was just like what Henry described," said Dutch. "People are very angry. They say that proves you and your brother murdered Mr. Fisher."

"This can't be happening," said Arch. "It's like a nightmare. First they keep me away from Henry. Now they claim he is saying terrible and false things. I haven't heard it from Henry's lips. I don't believe it."

171

"People can do terrible things to each other," said G.W. "You don't know what they did to Henry."

"Already men stop to ask me where you are, Arch," said Dutch. "Angry men who drink too much. There will be more men later on. It's not even dark yet. Too many people can find you here. It is better if you come home. You stay in Israel's room or we send Nellie to visit her mother and you stay in the room off the kitchen."

"Wait," said G.W. "It's better if I don't know exactly where Arch is. They'll ask me and I'd better be able to swear on the bible that I don't know."

Arch looked at G.W. with pain in his eyes.

"It's better for both of us," said G.W. "You're a white man and you've never seen what a mob can do to a black man, but I have. Things can be done to make any man talk. They can make me talk too, if they catch me, but I can't tell them what I don't know."

"I'm sorry, G.W.," said Arch.

"I'm sorry too, but you'd better get over feeling sorry for yourself if you want to survive this thing. Feel sorry for Henry if you want, but get ready to defend yourself against him and the men pulling his strings. Get angry. Get real angry. Get ready to strike back. If you don't you'll end up standing on a scaffold with a rope around your neck wondering what happened."

"Listen to him, Arch," said Dutch. "He knows. When I arrive first some people hear my accent. They laugh at me. They steal from me. They tell me go home, Dutch man. I am not Dutch man. I am a German. They act like I am not a man because I am foreigner. People can do this. If a mob comes they look for you; then they look for others not their color like G.W.; then they look for others not their religion; then they look for others not born in this country."

172

"You must find Mr. Lincoln for me, Dutch," said Arch.

"Yes, yes," said Dutch. "He is a good man. He will help."

"He even thinks us coloreds are people," said G.W.

"Now, you must go at once," said Dutch. "Take back streets. Don't stop. Mamma will know what to do when you get home."

"I'm gone.," said Arch. "Thank you both."

Arch slipped from the room and cautiously left the house.

"I'd better go too," said G.W. "If you don't see me around for the next few days don't worry. I'll be back."

"Do you have a safe place?" asked Dutch. "I could find a spot for you at home."

"No. I'd stick out like a lump of coal in a sugar tin. But thank you for the offer. I can go where they can't find me."

"Arch is a good man, said Dutch. "God help him. God help us all."

Dr. Merryman finally finished his careful search of the thicket.

He noted with surprise that it was afternoon and that he was hungry. He did not notice that his clothes were muddy and his hands were filthy. The few men still around the thicket were busily engaged in the poker game where the stakes had been creeping higher all day.

"You can go now," said Dr. Merryman. "I'm done here."

"Fine doctor," said a man trying to figure out if he should keep an ace kicker or throw away three cards in hopes of improving on a pair of jacks. The other men were occupied with similar concerns so nobody paid any particular attention when the doctor departed for town alone ,whistling happily.

At the millpond the spirits of the men were not as high. On the positive side was the fact that Porter and his men finished tracing the stream in both directions until they were well past the point the Trailors could have reached in the time they had to hide the body. They returned to help in the search of the pond. That allowed tired men to take a rest while others worked. The work was done in shifts.

On the negative side, the ground uncovered by the receding pond water was slimy, slippery and covered with smelly weeds, discarded trash, hungry leaches and desperate fish. Every foot had to be examined with care. The weeds and mud clung to the searchers with an unholy tenacity. Movement was laborious. Each step was accompanied by a loud sucking sound. Each step was accomplished only after the expenditure of much energy needed to escape the eagerly embracing mud. Refuse turned up in abundance but not clues. When the stream finally reached what Hitchcock claimed was its original size, the men trolled the water from the dam to the inlet channel with rakes, hoes and poles. It was all to no avail.

Late in the afternoon all the men pitched in to rebuild the dam to Hitchcock's exacting standards. All day Hitchcock had refused to help in the search. He claimed it was all a wild goose chase and that Arch Trailor would never be involved in a murder. His attitude did not make him any friends and his thanks for the rebuilding effort was minimal at best. The men headed toward town, dirty, sore, tired, hungry and irritable.

Wednesday, Evening June 16, 1841 Springfield, Illinois

Henry Trailor woke up again. He felt surprised that it was dark outside. He wondered how long he had slept.
"Mr. Douglas," he called, "what time is it? How long have I been asleep?"

"You're awake," said Douglas. "It's near about seven or so give or take an hour. I don't rightly know. I was sort of dozing my own self. I've got to get Mr. Lamborn and Mr. Martin. They wanted to know when you woke up again. Do you need anything?"

"Do I need anything?" asked Henry. "You never asked me that before."

"I'll be back soon," said Douglas.

Henry rubbed his chin. He was surprised to find that he was clean-shaven. He noted that his body and clothes were clean. Even the bedding had been changed.

In a few minutes the attorney general and the mayor returned with Douglas.

"I'm glad to see you had a good sleep," said Martin to Henry. "That's one of the benefits of a clear conscience, no doubt."

"I've written up everything that you told us," said Lamborn. "I'd like you to read it over and tell me if I have all the details correct. Take your time and go over it carefully."

He handed Henry a stack of papers.

"What did I tell you?" asked Henry.

Martin and Lamborn laughed.

"Didn't I tell you?" asked Martin. "He's become as big a joker as Mr. Lincoln."

"That is a good one, Henry," said Lamborn. "If the mayor here and I had not both heard it all from you at the same time I might almost think you were serious."

"In some ways, I can admire the loyalty you showed by trying to protect your brothers; even though they committed murder without your knowledge and then dragged you right into the middle of it," said Martin.

"I said that?" asked Henry.

"Yes, you finally broke down and told us the truth. We both heard you. It's all on the papers here. Just like you told us. Read them. They'll help you remember how it happened," said Lamborn.

"I remember some of this," said Henry reading the papers.

"Read it," said Lamborn. "Think about it. Remember how you felt about it. Picture it in your mind. It will become clear to you."

Dennis Kelly sat in the main room of Keys' tavern listening to the men around him. He smiled inwardly at the dark mood of the drinkers. While most of the men who actually spent the day searching were too tired to go out, the men in the tavern regaled each other with talk about how hard they had worked in the futile search. Each man tried to top the others including men Kelly personally knew had never set foot outside of town.

Kelly bought drinks for the loudest of the talkers to encourage them.

"I don't see why we have to bother with trial." Kelly. "It seems to me that the hangman shouldn't have all the fun."

Several men shouted in approval.

"What else do we need to know?" asked Kelly. "Henry Trailor confessed. We know where Arch Trailor lives. I say we pay him a visit, give him a ride on a rail and hold a rope party with Arch as the honorable guest."

"He's right!" shouted a man in the background.

"Let's get him," said another.

Men at the edge of the tavern ran off to invite their friends to the party. A small group of men surged out of the tavern. They were followed by another, larger group, who were not quite as bold as the first men. Someone in the street brought torches. With laughter and celebration the torches were lit. The men paraded past other taverns where the noise and excitement attracted others. Many men joined the crowd without knowing why it was gathering. Other men ran to tell the sheriff.

"Let's get that murderer," shouted someone. Some men hesitated or stopped but the rest of the men headed unsteadily toward the Myers boarding house in a mob.

Kelly stood in the darkness and watched the mob head off. Then he headed back to Keys' tavern. Edwin Brown, the bar tender was standing behind the bar.

"Give me a drink," said Kelly.

"Coming up," answered Brown. "I thought you'd be out leading the men toward Myers."

"Me?" asked Kelly. "I'm a law abiding soul."

"Didn't I hear you say something about a hanging?" asked Brown.

"Oh, that," said Kelly. "That was just the whiskey talking. I've always been a bit windy, but I mean no harm. When the sheriff comes around you can tell him I was in here. And I'll do the same for you."

Brown considered for a moment. The tavern was deserted except for two men who were passed out from drinking or else were sleeping at a table.

"I see what you mean," said Brown. "I've always been a peaceful man, myself."

"Where's Keys been these past few days?" asked Kelly.

"Lamborn and Martin sent him away on party business for a day or two." Brown. "If you want my opinion, I'd say they wanted him out if town so they could do what they needed to do without him looking over their shoulder."

"And Keys left you to watch the cash box? asked Kelly. "I thought he was smarter than that."

"Keys decided how much money should be in the box when he returns and how much *I* would pay *him* to keep bar while he is away," said Brown.

"Did he now?" asked Kelly. "How about a free drink in honor of absent friends?"

Kelly closed his eyes and felt the warmth of the drink traveling down his throat. He wondered how much of the Myers house would be left intact when the mob was through with it. He imagined that his former fellow boarders would try to defend Arch and fight off the mob. Maybe some of them would be hurt in the fight. He smiled to himself.

Sheriff Young ran through the dark streets of Springfield looking for Deputy Wickersham. He cursed himself for sending Jim Maxey instead of Alonzo Wickersham out of town to arrest William Trailor. Maxey could stand up to a mob without showing doubt or fear. He could back them down. Mr. Lincoln would not have tolerated a mob forming in Springfield. He would know how to make the men laugh and think about what they intended to do. He would have sent them off home to sober up. Young knew he alone could not back down a mob or joke with the men and send them off home. Young thought that if he found Wickersham in time there was still a chance that the two of them together could control the situation.

At Myers, Dutch and the boarders were expecting trouble. They had nailed all of the windows and every door, except the front door, shut. They had reinforced the front entryway just in case something like this happened. Leonard James and Elijah Hart would fight if anyone burst in trying to harm Arch. They armed themselves with staves and hammers. Although they were frightened, James Dorman and Samuel Franklin insisted on staying to help. It was not clear how much help they could give. Arch, himself, was shut into the narrow crawl space between the roof and the ceiling. The entry to the house from the crawl space was hidden and nailed shut from the inside of the crawl space. Arch had an unobtrusive exit to roof and strict instructions not to show himself regardless of what happened.

An unknown man came out of the darkness to warn the Myers that the mob was coming. He then slipped away saying he was looking for the sheriff and the deputy.

"I still say the best thing would be for me to talk with them alone, dear" said Mrs. Myers to her husband. "No sane man would offer violence to a woman in public."

"This is a mob, Momma," said Dutch. "They'll be drunk and wanting a show. They won't listen to you. You'd be one woman alone facing dozens of men."

"That's it exactly," said Mrs. Myers. "They'd be surprised. They wouldn't know what to do. They wouldn't be threatened or challenged like they might be if it were a man facing them. I could get them to stop for a moment. Then they would think and maybe to listen to me."

"Mamma, please," said Dutch, "I'm afraid you'd get hurt. I want you to visit Mrs. White where Israel and Nellie are now. I don't want you to be inside when the men come."

"Yes, dear," said Mrs. Myers. "I promise I will not be inside the house when the men arrive. In fact I'm leaving now." She kissed Dutch and stepped outside.

Dutch was momentarily puzzled by his wife's agreement. Even when he persuaded her to his point of view she rarely agreed so readily or so quickly. Maybe the danger of the situation made her unusually compliant.

"Dutch," called Franklin, "come tell me if you think this barricade is strong enough."

Dutch went to inspect the barricade. Elise Myers stood on the porch and idly picked up a broom Nellie had left there in her haste. In the distance she could see the torches of the approaching mob. Automatically she turned her back to the approaching mob and started to sweep the dusty porch vigorously sending clouds of dust into the air. The head of the mob reached the bottom of the steps and hesitated. They could see that she was alone on the porch. Mrs. Myers continued to sweep energetically.

"What is she doing?" Dutch asked James as they looked out a peephole.

"I don't know," said James. "Whatever it is it has quieted the mob. Stay here and let's see what happens." He put his strong hands on Dutch's shoulder. Although his grip was light, Dutch knew he could not pull away James, if James did not want him to.

Mrs. Myers studiously avoided looking in the direction of the men as she finished her sweeping. She picked up a small, carved wooden horse on wheels that Israel left on the porch. Then she turned around and pretended to see the men for the first time. She stepped back as if surprised and then stepped forward again holding the toy horse where the men could see it.

"Good evening, gentlemen," she said calmly.

The men in the front of the crowd milled about and looked for a leader. Finally one man cleared his throat.

"Good evening, Ma'am," said the man.

"I certainly hope all of you are not thinking of bringing your muddy shoes onto the porch I just swept," said Mrs. Myers.

"Uh, no Ma'am," said the man.

"Don't you think it's rather late to come calling?"

"Uh, yes Ma'am," said the man.

The men in the crowd shuffled around and talked quietly to each other.

"Is that Billy Herndon I see?" Mrs. Myers asked a young man in the crowd.

"Yes, Ma'am," said Billy. He removed his hat and moved to the front of the crowd.

"It is nice of you to come visit," said Mrs. Myers. "Unfortunately it is too late tonight. Why don't you come back tomorrow?"

"Yes, Ma'am," said Billy. "I reckon it is too late for any of us to be here." He turned and left. Several men in the back of the crowd started to drift away quietly. "If you're looking for room and board," said Mrs. Myers, "I don't have space for all of you. If you want to ask individually please come back in the morning, after breakfast."

Larger numbers of men broke off from the crowd and walked away. The men in the front of the group looked at each other and backed away.

"Beg your pardon, Ma'am," said the man who had spoken first.

"Have a good evening, sir."

"Thank you, Ma'am. You rest easy."

"I will now."

Sheriff Young finally found Wickersham. Together the men walked the streets and found that there was no disturbance. Just to be certain the peace would remain they went to every tavern in Springfield and ordered them to stop serving alcohol for the rest of the night. The rest of the night passed quietly.

Chapter Eighteen

Thursday, June 17, 1841 Springfield, Illinois

Very early in the morning a tall, lanky man came riding into town on a rough buggy pulled by a plodding, skinny, swayback horse. He noticed that the streets were deserted and unusually silent. He guided his horse to a livery stable. He removed the animal's often-mended harness. Then he let the animal into a stall making certain there was enough water and fodder available.

Manasseh Porter stumbled into the stable rubbing his bloodshot eyes.

"I'm sorry, Mr. Lincoln," he said. "Usually when somebody comes into the stable I hear the noise and come down right away. You didn't need to take care of your horse. I would have done that."

"That's all right, Manasseh," said Lincoln. "I still remember my way around a horse. That, there is the end that eats and this end here..."

"That, Mr. Lincoln is something a hostler knows all about."

"I apologize to you," said Lincoln, "I yield to your superior knowledge. But I assure you there are occasions on which an attorney deals with nearly as much manure as a hostler."

"You certainly have an ugly beast," said Porter.

"He suits me well. The horse and I the same kind of beast, ugly, slow, but useful. We plod along slowly, but steadily. Sooner or later, mostly later, we get there."

Porter laughed.

"You may say that when people see an ugly man on an ugly nag they think, "There goes an ugly pair. Well, think how it would be if I rode a handsome horse. It would make the horse look even more handsome, but I'd look even uglier."

"I can ill afford that," said Lincoln. "Why, just the month past when I was riding on the court circuit a woman saw me passing by and stopped me to complain that I was so ugly that I had ruined what had been a fine day for her. I protested that while it might be true, it was certainly not my fault. She thought for a moment and said 'But you could have stayed home.'"

Porter laughed again.

"It's good to have you back, Mr. Lincoln. There hasn't been much to laugh about here."

"I've heard rumors, but I didn't know how much to believe."

"Shoot, I've been in town the whole time and I don't know how much to believe either.," said Porter. "You can usually make sense of things. If I tell you what happened can you tell me what to think?"

"I'm not much on telling others what to think," said Lincoln. "On the other hand, it could be that telling me would help you figure out what you think on it. I admit I'm like the boy outside the circus tent, mighty curious about what's going on out of sight. How about you join me for breakfast and we'll go over the matter."

"That's all right by me," said Porter. "The thing I don't understand is that I've always thought of Arch Trailor as a man about as honest as the day is long. But after Henry's confession..."

"Whoa," said Lincoln holding up his palm. "Just pretend to be like my horse. Let's plod through this one step at a time. How did it start?"

"I guess it started when Asher Keys received a letter from the postmaster in Warren County."

"When was that?" asked Lincoln.

Let's see," said Porter, "It was Friday, I think. Yes, Friday. Just six days ago. It seems a lot longer than that. So much has happened."

"What exactly did this letter say?" asked Lincoln.

"They posted copies around town. I kept one I could show you."

"Excellent, if you don't mind getting one for me, that would be most helpful."

Slowly and carefully over breakfast, Lincoln took Porter through each day and each event. He asked questions but made no comments about the happenings.

"I heard there was a mob with torches that went looking for Arch last night," said   Porter. "I was so tired that I slept through most of it but Mr. Wickersham stopped by and told me about it later. It was mostly rowdies and drunks looking for some fun. Seems like once they got to the Myers they found Mrs. Myers outside sweeping her porch. She was polite to the men but scolded them for calling so late at night. There wasn't a man there who'd raise a hand against her, a respectable wife and mother. If anybody tried he would have been the one who ended up the one dancing on the end of a rope most likely.

"She warned them not to track up her clean porch with their muddy boots. She said if any man wanted to board there he should come back in the morning to talk about it. Then they went home to sleep it off, I guess."

"An admirable woman."

"Braver than the whole mob put together. I wonder what set them off. Now that I think about it I wonder several things."

"Like what?" asked Lincoln.

"Like what took Henry Trailor so long to confess.," said Porter. "Like how come he confessed that he didn't do the crime. You'd think a confession would mean that you admit you did it. His confession is that he didn't do it. I wonder that I ain't heard it from his own lips yet. I know some of the rumors are wrong. The Trailors never paid me in gold but as much as I say that the rumor keeps going around. It's like there's somebody saying it fresh all the time. I ain't saying I know as they didn't kill Mr. Fisher, but I surely don't know as they did. There's something strange about this."

"If the Trailor's asked you to testify that they didn't pay you in gold, would you say so under oath?"

"Sure, since it's so. I was thinking though, I might see about getting on the jury."

"That could happen." Lincoln. "You never know."

Lincoln walked through the still sleeping town until he arrived at this law office. He discovered several notes in the neat handwriting of his partner, Judge Logan. Deputy Wickersham had been by saying that Jack Armstrong was worried about his neighbor, Henry Trailor, current resident in the Springfield jail. Arch Trailor had been by several times on different days asking that Lincoln and Logan help get his brother, Arch out of jail, then asking if the lawyers could help him visit Henry, and finally asking if the lawyers would represent his brothers if there was a trial. Lincoln noted that, although the tone of the requests became more desperate as the days passed, Arch did not ask them to represent him. Arch did not seem to expect to be arrested. Edward D. Baker left his card with a brief note offering to join in the Trailors' defense if Logan and Lincoln wanted him to. Alternately he proposed to have them join him if the Trailors decided to apply to him for legal counsel.

It seemed to Lincoln that, whatever his wishes were, he would likely end up working on the case one way or another; *nolens volens*. Lincoln rested his chin on his fist and thought carefully about what Porter had told him.

A few hours later Jim Maxey led his charges into Springfield. He noticed that the people on the streets stopped to stare at the caravan. Some people looked hostile. Others looked sympathetic. Still others looked curious. Maxey wondered at the variety of facial expressions of the citizens of Springfield. He took William to the jail first.

"I'd appreciate it if all of you would wait for me outside," said Maxey. He addressed his remarks to the whole group but his eyes stayed on Cassandra.

"This shouldn't take long and I promise you can talk to him after he gets settled in," said Maxey. Maxey knew men sometimes reacted badly when facing the prospect of actually entering the jail. Some formerly quiet men fought like hungry wolves. Other men burst into tears and had to be reassured. He hoped to spare Cassandra any embarrassment.

William accepted being put in a cell calmly and without protest.

"Where's Henry Trailor?" Maxey asked Douglas.

"Mr. Lamborn decided to keep him at his house," said Douglas. "He said he didn't want Henry influenced by his brothers."

"How's that?" asked Maxey. "He's never done anything like that before."

"Well, after Henry confessed you can see how he'd want to keep the brothers apart," said Douglas.

"What's that?" asked Maxey. "Henry confessed and he's out of jail? William claims he's innocent and he's in jail? Did everybody in town go crazy while I was away?"

"Maybe so. Things have been strange around here. Henry confessed that Arch and William killed Mr. Fisher. He said he found out about it later."

"Where's Arch then?" asked Maxey.

"He's in town somewhere," answered Douglas. "Last night there was a mob looking for him but they didn't find him. They backed down when they got to the Myers."

"The sheriff and Alonzo told them off?" asked Maxey.

"No," said Douglas, smiling. "Mrs. Myers backed them up all by herself armed with a broom and a toy horse. The way I hear it the sheriff couldn't find Alonzo and he didn't hanker to face the mob all by himself. There's talk that someone in petticoats might be persuaded to run against him come next election."

Douglas slapped his knee and laughed at his own joke.

189

"I can see I shouldn't have left this town on its own," said Maxey. "Mr. Trailor's daughter will be coming over later to visit him. I'd appreciate it if you let them have some privacy."

"Is she a pretty one?" asked Douglas.

"I'd say so," answered Maxey. He left the jail and returned to the people waiting outside for him.

"Your father settled in easily," said Maxey to Cassandra. "He's calm and he didn't seem upset."

"He's too calm," said Cassandra. "Shouldn't a man facing a murder trial be upset?"

"I'd say so, Miss. Most men are."

"And my father is not," said Cassandra. "He smiles and goes along like his life is not at risk. When I try to talk to him about it he says that God will protect him. He's always been a religious man but he's never been so passive. I'm very concerned about him."

"I've never seen a man accused of murder act like your father does," admitted Maxey. "He's not trying to protect himself. I think you're going to have to act for him."

Cassandra nodded sadly.

"Gentlemen," said Maxey to George Digby, Alexander Baldwin, and Dr. Gilmore, "if you want to stay at a hotel there are several in town. If you want to stay at a boarding house I'm headed over to the Myers which I recommend highly. They may have a room for you Miss Trailor. I don't know."

"That's where my uncle Arch lives.," said Cassandra.

"I know," said Maxey. "I want to talk to him."

190

"So do I." Cassandra stuck out her chin.

Maxey recognized the sign that Cassandra had made up her mind to do something.

"That sounds good to me," said Dr. Gilmore. "Lead on."

Digby and Baldwin concurred.

At the Myers, Dutch, G.W., and Arch were busy removing barricades and taking down boards that had closed off the windows.

"It looks like you had the placed fortified for a siege," said Baldwin.

"We expected one," said Dutch, "But Mamma swept the mob away with her broom."

"Nonsense, father," said Mrs. Myers, "I knew the men would not dare attack a woman. Once they thought it over, they decided they were acting foolishly."

"Uncle Arch," said Cassandra. "I'm so glad to see you."

She ran to Arch and hugged him.

"Father is acting strangely," said Cassandra. "I don't understand what is going on."

"Nothing makes sense any more, said Arch. "Henry has gone crazy. He claims that William and I killed Mr. Fisher."

"That's impossible," said Cassandra. "Mr. Fisher is recovering from an illness at Dr. Gilmore's home."

"That's right," said Dr. Gilmore. "I've treated him for years when he's been ill. More often, of course since the accident."

"Do you hear that, Mother?" asked Dutch. "Mr. Fisher is alive."

"But he's not here," said Cassandra. "If Henry is telling people that Arch and my father killed Mr. Fisher what will people think?"

"If he recovers as quickly as he has in the past he may be able to travel slowly within a few days from now," said the doctor."

"You'll just have to go pick him up and bring him back, father," said Mrs. Myers. "That way people will know for certain that he was not killed."

"Who will protect Arch?" asked Dutch. "You can't stand guard with your broom every night, mother."

"I could take him to jail," said Maxey. "If there have been threats on your life, they should have taken you there before. I can't recommend the accommodations but I can promise you it'll be safe. You can talk with William. He's there."

"What about Henry?" asked Arch. "They haven't let me see him since he was arrested."

"I've heard he's somewhere else. He's safe anyway. I don't know what's been happening here because I've been out of town but I'm certainly going to find out."

"Do go with him, uncle," pleaded Cassandra. "You can trust him. Then I'll know you're safe and my father's safe."

"I will."

"I'll talk with Mr. Galaway to see if I can borrow his two horse carriage," said Dutch. "Maybe he'll come with me. We'll fetch the man from the doctor's house and bring him back as quick as wink."

"I'll draw you a map to my house," said Dr. Gilmore.

"All of you can stay with us." Mrs. Myers. "You can stay here too, Miss Trailor, if you don't mind sharing a room with, Nellie, the hired girl."

"I'd be delighted to stay," said Cassandra, "Please let me help around the house. I have to stay busy. If I have nothing to do I'll start to stew about the whole thing and worry myself silly."

"I can always use another pair of willing hands," said Mrs. Myers. She and Cassandra went into the house talking. Cassandra insisted on carrying her bag into the house herself.

Dutch got directions and a quickly sketched map from the doctor. Then he hurried away. Maxey helped G.W. and Arch remove the last of the wooden fortifications from the house. Then he and Arch walked over to the jail. Some people stared angrily at Arch. Others seemed friendly and waved to him.

"People don't know what to think.," said Maxey.

"I hardly know myself," answered Arch.

William seemed happy to see Arch. He made no reference to their being in jail and when Arch brought it up William seemed blissfully unconcerned with their surroundings. Before he left the jail, Maxey promised Arch that he would ask Lincoln and Logan to stop by the jail.

"Pap, do you know where I can find Sheriff Young?" asked Maxey

"No. He hasn't been to the jail for a week or so."

193

Maxey nodded grimly. He had one stop to make before he went to the attorneys' office. He tracked the sheriff down in his office across the street from the jail.

"Jim," said the sheriff. "When did you get in? Sit down and talk to me."

Maxey remained standing.

"What the hell is going on?" he asked.

"What do you mean?" asked Young. "I haven't done anything."

"That's exactly what I mean. Arch Trailor asked to see his brother in jail and you did nothing. The attorney general and the mayor questioned a man in your jail for days on end and you did nothing. You didn't even show up there. A man's life was threatened and you did nothing to see that he was safe. A lynch mob walked the streets of the city and you did nothing."

Young squirmed but said nothing.

"There was a time when you were a big man in this town. A time where you didn't let things like those happen. I don't know what happened to you but you've been getting smaller lately. Pretty soon you'll be so small that there'll be nothing of you left."

Maxey turned and walked out.

"Jim," called Young. "Deputy Maxey, come back here."

Maxey ignored him and continued to walk. He knew he might have walked himself out of a job but at the moment he did not care. Maxey walked the streets of Springfield not paying attention to where he was going. He thought about the times in the past when the sheriff had been a man to count on. He wondered when and why that had started to change. When Maxey looked around he saw that he had come to Hoffman's Row. Maxey thought to himself that whether or not he had a job he had made a promise to Arch. He went to the office of Logan and Lincoln and knocked on the door.

"Come in," came a voice.

Maxey entered the office.

Abraham Lincoln was stretched out awkwardly over a chair with his legs resting on his desk.

"Mr. Lincoln, Arch Trailor is asking to see you. He's in jail charged with the murder of Mr. Fisher."

"Thank you, Mr. Maxey," said Lincoln. "Although to be honest I didn't really want to hear that. If Arch asks me to represent him, as I expect he will, he puts his life in my hands. That's a heavy responsibility."

"Well, I didn't want to arrest him either, but I did," said Maxie. "At least he's safe now. That might be the only thing about this whole case that I can be proud of. After you talk to Arch you might want to stop by the Myers. There's the postmaster from Warren County staying there who says he now knows that what he said in his letter proved to be rumors."

"He might be some help," admitted Lincoln.

"The farmer who sold his farm to William Trailor for hard cash is there too." Maxey.

"He could be useful too, I suppose," said Lincoln. "Maybe."

"As long as you're there, you might want to talk with Dr. Gilmore too."

"What does he say?" asked Lincoln.

"He says Archibald Fisher is alive."

Lincoln sat bolt upright.

"You wouldn't joke with me," said Lincoln.

"Not about a man's life."

"After I talk with them. I want to talk with you too."

After Dutch and Maxey left Cassandra and Mrs. Myers talked in the kitchen as they washed and dried the dishes left from breakfast. Nellie, the hired girl carried the dishes in from the breakfast table. Nellie was a shy, pretty young girl with curly brown hair and amber eyes. She lingered in the kitchen when she brought the dishes in. When she left to get more plates she returned very quickly.

"It was kind of you to send your husband to bring back Mr. Fisher," said   Cassandra. "Thank you."

"You're welcome. He was about to think of it for himself. I just speeded things up."

"Uncle Arch has told us how nice you and your husband were to him."

"He's a good man.," said Mrs. Myers. "Don't you think so, Nellie?"

Nellie, who had been moving slowly toward the door, scurried quickly from the room. Her cheeks had turned flaming red.

"I gather that Nellie is fond of your uncle," said Mrs. Myers, "not that he has noticed."

"Men can be so obtuse," said Cassandra. "Even if the moment is awkward."

Mrs. Myers paused for a moment and looked at Cassandra speculatively. Then she resumed washing.

"There are many people who think that there are too many immigrants in this country," said Mrs. Myers. "They claim the immigrants are ruining the country, not learning to speak English, and other foolishness. Your uncle came to work for my husband without prejudice or reservation. With him as a partner, more people use the business than ever before. He does more than his share of work. He helps us at least as much as we help him."

Nellie carried another load of dishes into the kitchen. Her cheeks were still pink. Then she turned and fled.

"Poor girl," said Mrs. Myers. "She wants to let Arch know how she feels but she doesn't know quite how. I think that after we finish here we should go do the shopping. Yes, that would be a good idea. We'll visit several stores. We'll look in at the milliner's and the dressmaker's. I'll introduce you as William Trailor's daughter. People will be ever so curious. They'll ask all sorts of questions. Then you can tell them that Mr. Fisher is alive and at a doctor's house. That's the best way to get the news out that Mr. Fisher is still alive. We need to get that news around the town as quickly as possible."

"Will you come with me to the jail after that?" asked Cassandra.

"Of course I will," answered Mrs. Myers.

When Lincoln arrived at the jail he found that Cassandra was visiting her father and uncle. Mrs. Myers was there too.

"Mrs. Myers." Lincoln tipped his hat. "Miss."

Mrs. Myers nodded pleasantly. Cassandra looked at him hopefully.

"Mr. Lincoln," said Arch, "thank you for coming."

"You're welcome, Arch. Should I come back later?"

"No. Please stay."

"Should we leave?" asked Mrs. Myers.

"For my part you're welcome to stay," said Arch. "What do you say, William? Mr. Lincoln?"

"It won't make any difference, " said William. "It's all in the Lord's hands."

"It's up to you gentlemen," said Lincoln. "I'm here at your request."

"Then please stay," said Arch. "We're all family or friends and we have no secrets here."

"How can I help you gentlemen?" asked Lincoln.

"I'd like you to represent us in court," said Arch.

"Well," you know there's lots of more experienced lawyers. I'm a self-taught attorney. There are many lawyers who have a better grasp of legal precedent and case law. Some know the statutes better than I do. Are you sure it's me you want?"

"Have you handled murder cases before?" asked Cassandra.

"Well, yes." admitted Lincoln.

"And you've won," Mrs. Myers.

"Not every time," said Lincoln. "Two years ago I defended William Fraim. He was found guilty and hanged. I might have gotten him off with a prison term except that the jury reckoned that he made a cold-blooded decision to kill a man rather than repay him the money he was owed. If he had killed the man in the heat of anger, or during a dust up or while drunk the jury might have been more sympathetic. Lots of men have done stupid things while angry and drunk but few are venal to the point of murder."

"You know me," said Arch. "Do you think I would kill a man for his money?"

"No, I don't reckon you would, But..."

"We're not poor," said Cassandra. "If that's what you're worried about."

"No Miss," said Lincoln. "I'm not a member of the law firm "Catch 'em and Cheat 'em" although I know some lawyers who are. I'm reluctant because I would fear to fail you. With lives on the line I worry that you might do better elsewhere."

"I'd say that speaks well of you," said Mrs. Myers. "I think you'll do all that you can to help."

"That's so. Do I have your permission to bring in Mr. Logan, my senior partner? He was a judge until he decided he'd rather practice law than judge it. He's an expert on procedure and laws. Also, I'd like to bring in Mr. Baker. He's a wonderful speaker and he has a first rate legal mind. With those two to back me up I reckon we could match Mr. Lamborn."

"I agree," said Arch.

"Now hold your horses," said William. "I need ask Mr. Lincoln some questions. I've heard some things about you that make me wonder if you are a sound man."

"Fire away."

"I hear you are not a member of a church. Are you an unbeliever?"

"No sir, " said Lincoln. "I am not a member of a church but I am a believer. I'm not much of a man for joining with groups of people. If I could find a church that had "Love and honor God" and "Love your neighbor as yourself" as the only tenets, I might join that church."

"Very well. I accept that. But I hear that you are not a temperance man either," said William.

"That's true. I'm not a man for taking oaths. It's also true that I don't drink alcohol. I don't even smoke. Although I admit I have been told that a man like me, without such vices, can be expected to have plaguey few virtues."

"I find nothing to criticize in your behavior," said William. "Although you lack seriousness. I also hear that earlier this year you lay in bed for a week although you did not have an illness."

"That is true," said Lincoln. "When my engagement to be married ended I was taken sorely with the hypo. For a week I questioned whether there was a purpose to my existence and whether I would ever be able to fulfill the responsibilities of a husband and father. After a week, I determined that I would never find the answers to those questions while I lay abed. So I returned to life, so to speak, and I am still seeking answers."

"That, at least, you take seriously," said William. "Please explain to me why you are not an abolitionist even though you accept that slavery is evil."

"Slavery, sir, existed before this country did. If the founding fathers, Washington, Jefferson and Madison all accepted its existence why can't we? Still, it is an evil beyond question. Earlier this year I traveled on a steamboat and saw manacled slaves chained together on their way south. Ever since then, I have been unable to remove that image from my mind. I own some uneasiness that the evil has not been removed from the country I honor, but where it exists our countrymen will not accept its abolition. I believe that the laws allowing slavery are unholy and they must, somehow be changed. Until then, sorrowfully but firmly, we must abide by the laws that exist."

"I am less than fully satisfied with your answer," said William.

"In truth, so am I. It is a troublesome question that divides us from our neighbors without clear resolution. If anyone can propose a remedy I would be disposed to listen."

"I have heard that you sometimes tell stories that can not be repeated to the ladies."

"To that I plead guilty. Especially if they are good stories. However, I do not tell them when there are ladies present. And I would ask, sir, if you have not done the same. Most farmers I know have a goodly supply."

"I have done the same," admitted William. "In my life I have committed many other sins and errors. I have come to believe that this trial to come will be a judgment of God upon me. Therefore I don't see the need for earthly counsel. Please understand Mr. Lincoln I believe you are a good man. Flawed and imperfect but a good man all the same. I am innocent of the particular charge against me but I am not looking for a defender. Since this ordeal began, I have been scorned and abused. The wickedness of the world weighs heavily upon me and I seek no shelter except God's love."

William folded his hands, bowed his head and closed his eyes. He seemed lost to the world.

"Poor father," whispered Cassandra. "Mr. Lincoln you see why I worry about him. He won't stand up for himself even though the charges are false."

"Will he let me represent him?" asked Lincoln.

"I can convince him," said Cassandra. "He wouldn't want his children to have it said about them that their father is a murderer."

"If you can not represent him; represent me," said Arch. "If William does not hang because I'm proved innocent, (so William must be innocent too.) His conscience will just have to bear it."

"I won't be able to put him on the stand," cautioned Lincoln. "He sounds guilty of something. Arch, tell me everything you can remember about the days your brothers and Mr. Fisher were in town. Start at the beginning and go slowly."

Chapter Nineteen

Friday, June 18, 1841 Springfield, Illinois

The Christian Church used as a courthouse was thronged with people hours before the trail was scheduled to start. The sanctified surroundings had no visible effect on the behavior of the noisy excited crowd. Tobacco was smoked or chewed and spit with abandon. Liquor of all sorts was imbibed openly. Muddy boot prints and tobacco stains were clear all over the floor. People who had arrived early conducted spirited bidding for the seats they held as it got closer to the time of the anticipated action. Well-dressed ladies sat demurely with their escorts but their eager eyes showed the level of interest that the proceeding held.

Rumors flowed from one end of the room to the other and then back again. The rumors were so changed in the process that they arrived back at their starting place as brand new rumors. Among the more colorful rumors were: A gang of heavily armed and rough looking men had been overheard plotting the armed escape of the Trailors. The Trailors were already dead having committed suicide out of remorse the night before. The ghost of Archibald Fisher had been seen walking over the surface of the millpond. Fisher was in town in disguise as a woman; he hated the Trailors and only pretended to disappear; he would reappear after they were hung to dance over their graves. Every lawyer in town refused to defend the Trailors because ministers had advised them that to do so would put their immortal souls in peril.

Heated debate raged about Dr. Gilmore. Some claimed he was obviously a lair. Others said he was a deluded former buffalo hunter. Still others whispered that he was the brains behind a whole series of murders for profit originating from the gangs of New York. Yet another group of people strongly argued that there was no reason at all for a trial since Mr. Fisher was not found alive.

Mary Todd, a short, pleasingly plump, pretty woman, with flawless pale skin, bright blue eyes and well arranged chestnut hair, was dressed in latest fashion. She stood on her tiptoes in a vain attempt to see over the crowd and locate empty seats. Next to her stood her friend Julia Jayne. Julia was an inch or so taller than Mary Todd. She was plump and blond and very nearly as pretty. She was much better dressed than most of the people in the crowd. Her efforts seemed aimed at avoiding contact with the people around her and seeking an exit path from the building.

"Mary, there's no place to sit and we have no escorts," said Julia. "'Tisn't proper for unmarried women to be in a place like this without an escort. We'll have to leave. I don't know how I let you drag me into this in the first place."

Mary pretended not to hear as she scanned the area for possible seats. She was worried. If Julia actually started to leave it would be socially impossible for her to stay by herself. Her current behavior, trying to attend the trial with only an unmarried woman as an escort, was already well outside what was expected of women of her status. She could have requested a male escort as society expected but she knew her guardian, Mr. Ninian Edwards, would surely have refused to allow her near the trial. Therefore she simply told him she would be going out with Julia. He was too disinterested to ask questions, so he had not found out her intentions and therefore had not formally forbidden her attendance.

"Miss Todd, Miss Jayne," came a friendly but unfamiliar female voice.

Mary's sharp eyes spotted a competent looking blond woman dressed modestly and waving to them. Next to her sat a pretty young woman of little distinction. On the other side, sat a more distinctive young woman with hair the color of coppery gold. Mary thought the blond woman looked slightly familiar although she doubted they had been formally introduced. The other two women were strangers to her. Mary steered her reluctant friend through the mass of people in the woman's direction.

"I'm Mrs. Dutch Myers," said the woman. "You can call me Elise. We haven't met, formally I mean, but I have seen you around Springfield. My husband is away on a critical task so I have no proper escort. I wonder if you two ladies would do me the great favor of sitting with me to avoid the unpleasant talk that might occur if I were to stay here with only my young friends Nellie and Cassandra."

"I don't ..." started Julia.

"Of course." Mary maneuvered herself deftly next to Mrs. Myers. "We could hardly refuse to assist a woman in such straits. It is our Christian duty to help others when we can, Julia."

Two men who had been sitting in the same pew as Mrs. Myers rose and touched their hats before moving off into the crowd to make room for Mary and Julia.

"Thank you gentlemen." Mary sat down. "You'd better sit down, Julia. There's such a crowd that if you don't sit immediately someone will take your place."

Recognizing that she had been outflanked once again by her quick-witted friend Julia sat.

"Before I forget my manners completely," said Mary, "I should formally introduce myself and my friend, even though you know our names. I'm Mary Todd. This is my friend Julia Jayne."

"I'm pleased to meet you," said Mrs. Myers. "Nellie Caldwell here is the hired girl at my boarding house. Cassandra Trailor is a visitor with a particular interest in the trail. We thank you for your help."

Mary looked at Cassandra and then at Mrs. Myers with her eyes sparkling. Her curiosity about Cassandra showed in her eyes but she was too well bred to ask the questions that immediately came to her mind.

"It helps us too," said Mary. "Why, we were just thinking that we might have to depart if we could not find appropriate companions."

Julia's look at Mary came perilously close to an impolite stare.

In a far corner of the room Jim Maxey looked longingly at Cassandra Trailor. Alonzo Wickersham came up to him smiling.

"Mr. Maxey," said Wickersham, "I'm glad to see you back here. We've certainly needed your help."

"From what I've heard you've done exceptionally well while I was gone. You brought in Henry Trailor without embarrassing him, or yourself. You defused the situation at the millpond that could have become a lynching. You closed down the taverns with the sheriff when the situation in town got ugly. I'd say you didn't need me at all."

"I didn't reckon that Arch needed arresting." Wickersham. "You would have known that. Lucky for me that Mrs. Myers was smart and brave enough to handle that."

"Lucky for all of us. If the sheriff had done his job none of this would have happened. But you, my young friend, have proved to be a real deputy. If I quit this job I'll know that I leave it in good hands."

"You wouldn't quit," protested Wickersham. "You haven't taught me even a quarter of what I need to know."

"I might quit," said Maxey. "I haven't decided yet. I don't think I'll be able to work for Mr. Young much longer. What he's been doing stinks like week old fish. I knew about some of that, not much but some, and I didn't object. So some little bit of that stink is rightly mine. When a man begins to smell in his own nostrils it's time for him to change what he's doing."

"Don't be too hasty." said Wickersham. "I too had some idea something was not right."

"You hadn't been a deputy very long. You weren't in a position to say much. I was. Anyway I won't be deciding anything right away. It's going to be a pleasure to work with you in the meantime."

"Thank you."   Wickersham blushed.

Maxey nodded. "I don't like the look of that group of men," he said pointing. "Let's have a palaver."

The group included Kelly, Brown, and others known to Maxey as rowdies. They sat in the middle of the room drinking from jugs, talking loudly and making rude remarks to the people unfortunate enough to be sitting close to them. Maxey approached at an angle to avoid drawing attention to himself. He motioned Wickersham to stay behind him. Maxey noted that one of the men kept playing with something and Kelly kept telling the man to leave it alone. As he got closer, Maxey saw that it was a noose.

"All right," said Maxey,. "That's enough. All of you get out of here."

"We've been waiting all morning," complained Brown. "You can't just up and toss us out."

"I just did.," said Maxey. The men hesitated. Wickersham came up to stand next to Maxey. Sullenly, the men stood and muttering curses. they moved from the pew. As Kelly passed Wickersham, he noted that Wickersham was looking at a man who refused to stand up. Maxey was standing a few steps away. Kelly raised his hand with a whiskey bottle in it. Then, Maxey's fist caught him solidly on the ear. Kelly dropped the bottle. He fell face first to the ground smashing the bottle underneath him. Kelly's face was cut and bleeding from the glass when Maxey hauled him unceremoniously erect. The whiskey from the bottle stung in Kelly's cuts and his eyes watered from the pain.

"I'm bleeding," said Kelly.

"You'd better be out of town by the time I get out of the trial, or you'll bleed a lot more," said Maxey. "I'll come looking for you. You better not be here. If I didn't have to stay here now I'd run you in for attacking a deputy and you'd be the next one up in court." Maxey shoved Kelly in the direction of the door. Kelly stumbled and nearly fell. He beat a hasty retreat from the church. The man who had been reluctant to get up looked at Maxey's unwavering stare. He rose quickly and hurried toward the exit.

"Thanks, Mr. Maxey." said Wickersham.

"It's the cowards you've got to watch out for.," said Maxey. "They strike when they think you're not paying attention. They're like snakes. Springfield will be better off without him."

"I think I'll talk to Brown when this is over," said Wickersham. "He's the same type."

"I accept the jury as it stands." Lamborn.

"Mr. Lincoln," said Lavely. "Tis your turn."

Lincoln rose and crossed over to the jury. He stood for a few minutes with his arms held behind his back, his left hand held in his right, looking at the men in the jury.

"Good morning, gentlemen" said Lincoln in his high pitched voice.

"Good morning," answered the jury.

"You heard Mr. Lamborn refer to this as a uniquely American drama." Lincoln. "That's a good description of what goes on here. Mr. Lamborn is a very fine lawyer. My role in this drama is that of defender. I represent the accused men in the particular. In the general case, I represent the people as much as Mr. Lamborn does. In the American system any man may be accused. If accused, that man is entitled to a number of things. He is entitled to a vigorous defense. He is entitled to a fair trial with a judge, or judges, to insure that the contest is fair. And he is entitled to one more thing. He is entitled to a presumption of innocence. No matter what is before a trial starts or what is done to make him look guilty. When the trial starts he starts off clean. He is judged to be guilty of no crime unless it is proved and proved beyond a reasonable doubt he is guilty. In this uniquely American system it is you, the jury, who makes that determination. We may thunder or implore. We may object or plead but it you who decide."

"I wonder how many of you were engaged in searching for Mr. Fisher's body?"

Ten of the twelve men held up their hands.

"Mr. Platt," said Lincoln. "You were not involved?"

219

"I had a fever. The doctor wouldn't let me."

"Mr. Johnson. why didn't you get involved?"

"I was out of town for most of the time or I would have been." answered Johnson.

"Mr. Lincoln," said May, "you may approach the bench with opposing counsel."

Lincoln and Lamborn walked over to the judges.

"Mr. Lincoln," said Lavely, "if it was your intention to demonstrate how the jurors in this case were heavily involved in the search, you have done that. We would allow dismissal of all ten for cause. Maybe all twelve."

"We would still probably look favorably on a request for a change of venue and a delay," added May.

"May I could consult with my colleagues?" asked Lincoln. He went over to the defense table and conversed with Logan and Baker briefly before returning to the judges.

"I would like to thank your honors for the kind advice," said Lincoln,. "However, we would like to proceed with the questioning of the potential jurors and the trail at this time."

"Very Well," said Lavely

"I hope you know what you're doing, Mr. Lincoln.," said May.

"I pray to God that I do."

Lincoln looked at each man in turn.

"All of you have already labored to find the truth in this case," said Lincoln. "Is there any man among you who thinks that just because he labored there must have been a crime committed? Is there any man here who thinks just because he and others have labored he can not dismiss the charges against my clients if there is not proof; and proof at a level that reaches beyond a reasonable doubt?"

Lincoln paused and looked at each man in the jury again in turn. "We accept the jury as presently constituted."

"Mr. Lamborn, said May, "you may make your opening statement."

"Thank you, your honors Gentlemen, on behalf of the people I would like to thank you for the time and attention you will spend on this matter. As my esteemed colleague, Mr. Lincoln, pointed out I should thank you for the time and effort you have already spent on this."

Lamborn started in a somber voice.

"The matter before us is both grave and grim. It is no less than the unlawful taking of a life. Murder. Criminal execution. Assassination. The reason for this heinous crime against man and God? No more reason than to gain financially. The bible tells us that the desire for money is the root of all evil. And so it was, here."

Lamborn shook his head as if sad.

"We will demonstrate that the vicious act of murder was committed by Arch Trailor and his brother William Trailor. We will show that the act was carefully planned. We will show that it was carried out in a calculated and cold-blooded fashion; like something we would expect from a wild beast rather than from a human being. We will show that a man who lived among us showing the shape of a man but underneath the shape of a man was the cunning and cruelty of a wild beast, a wolf thirsting for gold. The soulless beast was willing to take any step, no matter how depraved, to feed that unholy desire."

Lamborn pointed at the Trailors sitting at the defense table.

"Liar," whispered Nellie fiercely. Her face contorted in anger. Mrs. Myers looked at her sympathetically. "I'm afraid, Nellie, you may hear even worse things."

"We will demonstrate that on Monday, May 31st of this year while William and Henry as well as Mr. Fisher were purportedly visiting Arch in Springfield, and unknown at the time to Henry Trailor, William and Henry did with evil intent lure Mr. Fisher to a thicket northwest of town. Therein William cruelly struck him with a club and Arch viciously choked him until he lay dead upon the ground. These two villains, fiends masquerading as human men, did then leave the body of Mr. Fisher exposed to the elements. That night and in the morning, and yet again after dinner, Arch and William Trailor organized counterfeit searches of the city. While they were secretly laughing Henry was actually searching for Mr. Fisher.

"Although there were remonstrations against William's plans, he left the next day, Tuesday June 1. He knew well that Mr. Fisher would not ever need transportation from him again. We will show that William and Henry did leave town by a route that would not take them to their destinations. We will show that after leaving town William and Henry were joined by Arch. Henry was left as a sentry while William and Henry lifted the dead body of Mr. Fisher from the thicket where they had left him.

"William and Henry carried the body away in the dearborn in the direction of the mill pond. After a time they returned without the body. They told Henry they had taken care of *him*. You will hear respectable people tell you under oath that William and Henry returned from their deathly detour to Springfield. Then they struck out again. William and Henry returned to their homes while Arch resumed his false facade living within the bosom of our fair community as if the foul deed had not been done.

Lamborn scowled. "It is beyond endurance that we in the great state capital have been duped, bamboozled and veritably skinned alive by these, these demons in human form. We have been made a laughing stock by the actions of these men. Our reputation has been besmirched. We must regain our respect. We can not allow the spawn of Satan to go away unscathed."

Lamborn paused and looked expectantly at the crowd. There was silence. People looked around at each other puzzled. After a moment Lamborn resumed his oration.

"At the time, we in Springfield knew nothing of the crime that had been perpetrated but the arrogance of these evil men and their contempt for all they we hold dear could not, in the end, be contained. Just as some people beam with the light of honor which ultimately shine forth, others have the stench of brimstone about them, which can not forever be concealed. In this particular, we received in Springfield a letter from the postmaster of Warren County. He pointed the way. You will hear from him how William boasted of inheriting money from Mr. Fisher, how he spent unexplained gold coin and how he was denounced from the pulpit by his own minister.

"You will hear about the search for clues and how the very spot described by Henry Trailor yielded mute but none the less, telling evidence of the callous crime perpetrated there. You will hear of other indications that the evildoers were not able to cover up. You will see how the trail leads slowly but inexorably to the bloody handed murderers Arch Trailor and his brother William Trailor."

Lamborn gave a shuddering sigh and wiped his brow with his handkerchief. "Thank you for your close attention." He sat down.

"Mr. Lincoln," said May, "you may give your opening statement."

Lincoln stood and walked toward the jury. He leaned awkwardly forward with his right hand holding his left behind his back.

"Your honors, gentleman. I hope you listened closely to the statement of the attorney general I hope you will bear it in mind during the trial.

"If you do pay attention during the trial you will see that the prosecution will be unable to carry the burdens he has set out for himself. He must, and this is crucial, prove that there was a crime committed. Then he must, with no witnesses, prove that Arch and William committed it. If there is any reasonable doubt that there was a crime or that if there was a crime that Arch and William Trailor committed it, then you must acquit these men. Please bear in mind that the defense does not have to prove their innocence. We do not have to prove anything."

Lincoln walked back toward the table and then stopped. "If the attorney general agrees, this being a church we could find holy water and sprinkle it on the Trailors. I'll wager neither one of them vanishes in puff of smoke."

The jurors and the crowd laughed.

"Mr. Lamborn call your first witness," said Lavely.

Chapter Twenty One

Friday, June 18, 1841 Springfield, Illinois

"I call Mr. Alexander Baldwin," said Lamborn.

After Baldwin was sworn in the questioning started.

"Mr. Baldwin, can you tell us your residence and employment?"

"I live in Warren County, Illinois.," said Baldwin. "I own and run a tavern. Also, I am postmaster for Warren County."

"Did you send this letter to the postmaster of Springfield?" asked Lamborn handing him a sheet of paper.

Baldwin read the paper carefully then he answered. "Yes."

Lamborn took the paper to the bench and said, "I would like to have this letter entered into evidence, your honors."

"Mr. Lincoln what do you say?" asked Lavely.

Lincoln spoke briefly with Logan and Baker before responding.

"We're in something of a quandary here, your honors," said Lincoln. "The letter contains unsubstantiated rumor and gossip not ordinarily admitted in a court. On the other hand, everyone here in the courtroom has read it or at least heard about it. That makes it difficult to ignore. It's sort of like we're driving a heavy wagon and there is a deep mud hole in the main road. Even if we don't talk about it, we have to steer around it or face the consequences. Spoken about

225

or not, it effects what we do. On the whole, my learned colleagues and I think it would be better to have it on record, but we'd like to ask your honors for some leeway in questioning the author."

May and Lavely conferred. "That seems reasonable to us.." said May. "Mr. Lamborn you may have the letter admitted with the understanding that Mr. Trailor's counsel may have some room to ask questions in."

"I agree, sirs," answered Lamborn.

"Mr. Baldwin, did you write and send that letter?"

"Yes sir."

"Did you state in the letter that William Trailor traveled to Springfield with Mr. Fisher. That he returned alone and that Mr. Fisher's location was now unknown?" asked Lamborn.

"Yes sir. I did."

"Did you further state that Mr. Trailor refused to give an adequate explanation of Fisher's whereabouts?"

"I did," said Baldwin.

"Did you state that Mr. Fisher bought a farm with gold coin? That he was not known to have any gold before but that Mr. Fisher was locally thought to have wealth in the form of gold coins?"

"Yes sir." .

"Did you say that William Trailor was denounced from the pulpit of his church?" asked Lamborn.

"I did, sir."

"I'd say he was likely as poor as a preacher's thirteenth child," said

Baldwin.

"There were rumors of gold coins and such," said Lincoln. "Why do you think he was poor?"

"He didn't own much," said Baldwin. "He had a horse so skinny it wouldn't fill up a buzzard. He mostly worked for room and board. I never did think he had extra two bits. He hardly ever drank in the tavern unless somebody else was buying. He drank quick enough then. How was he supposed to carry all this gold around with him? Or did he have it buried in a treasure chest like the children thought?"

"When was the last time you laid eyes on Mr. Fisher?" asked Lincoln.

"I think a week or two before he went to Springfield." said Baldwin.

"Thank you, Mr. Baldwin. I have no further questions at this time."

The next witness was George Digby.

"Mr. Digby," said Lamborn, "You owned the farm next to William Trailor?"

"I did." .

"You sold the farm to him after he returned from Springfield in June of this year?"

"I did."

"Was the payment made in silver and gold coins?" asked Lamborn.

"It was."

"Had you seen Mr. William Trailor with gold and silver coins before the sale? asked Lamborn.

"I had not."

"Your witness, Mr. Lincoln."

"Good morning, Mr. Digby."

"Good morning, Mr. Lincoln."

"How long have you been Mr. Trailor's neighbor?" asked Lincoln.

"Oh, I'd say maybe fifteen years."

"And when did Mr. Trailor first express interest in buying your farm?" asked Lincoln.

"Maybe seven or eight years ago."

"So he didn't seem to be in any hurry about buying it," said Lincoln.

"No sir. I wasn't in a hurry about selling either."

"Who was it that first talked about his paying with hard cash?" asked Lincoln.

"I reckon it was me. I had some money in currency from a local bank that went belly up some years back. I told William if he wanted to buy my farm I'd give him a better price for payment in gold and silver."

"When was that?" asked Lincoln.

"When we were first starting to talk about it seven or eight years ago."

"Did Mr. Trailor tell you, seven or eight years ago, that he had hard cash?" asked Lincoln

"He said he had enough to match my price."   Digby.

"Thank you, Mr. Digby."

"Mr. Digby, did you actually see the money at that time?" asked Lamborn

"No sir, I did not."

"Mr. Digby, was it the habit in Warren County for men to go around showing their money to each other?" asked Lincoln.

"No sir."

"After you received the cash from Mr. Trailor, did you run about the county carrying the money to show it to others?" asked Lincoln.

"No sir."

"So in Warren County, a man might have money and choose not to show it off to others?"

""Yes sir."

"That's reassuring. After Mr. Lamborn's questions, I thought you might have different customs in Warren County than we have here," said Lincoln.

A ripple of laughter went through the audience. Even the judges smiled.

"Objection. Mr. Lincoln is making an argument. He is not asking questions."

"I'll withdraw it then," said Lincoln. "During the time that you were his neighbor, did you ever know Mr. Trailor to claim something to be true when it was false?"

"No sir."

"When did you last see Mr. Fisher?" asked Lincoln.

"The day he left for Springfield with Mr. Trailor."

"Thank you again, sir," said Lincoln. "I have no further questions for you at this time."

Mary Todd looked at her friend Julia. "When Mr. Lincoln starts to talk, you can quite forget his homely appearance and notice only his words."

"The appearance of a man hardly matters anyway," said Julia. "Kindness is much more important to a woman. And much more harder to find than a handsome face."

Mary turned to Mrs. Myers. "Mr. Lincoln did well there, don't you think?"

"Yes.. Mr. Lamborn overreached himself with those witnesses. It was not the first impression he wanted leave with the jury."

"I fear what comes next, though," said Cassandra.

"For the next witness, I'd like to call Mrs. Albert Thompson," said Lamborn.

Mrs. Thompson was a stately woman on middle years. She sat in the chair with her back erect and regarded the attorney general with something less than complete approval.

"Mrs. Thompson," can you tell the court what you saw of the Trailors early in the evening of the 31st of May?"

"I saw Arch Trailor, who I have often seen before, enter the woods to the north and west of town with two other men."

"Where did these men enter the woods?" asked Lamborn.

"It was past the road to Clary's Grove along another road," answered Mrs. Thompson.

"You have identified Arch as one of these men. Do you see anyone in the court who accompanied him?"

Mrs. Thompson peered around the church and then pointed toward William. "I believe that men there was one of them," she said. "I don't see the other man."

"Can you describe the third man?" asked Lamborn.

"He looked to be an older man than the other two. He had black hair with white shot through it. He was thin and wiry. I had not seen him before."

235

"Can you tell us what you saw after that?" asked Lamborn.

"After a hour or so, I didn't look at a clock. I saw Arch and that man, I think, return from the woods alone. As I was half way thinking the other man would be along I sort of kept a watch, but nobody else came from the woods that I saw."

"Your witness, Mr. Lincoln," said Lamborn.

Lincoln arose and approached the witness.

"Good Morning, Mrs. Thompson."

"Good Morning, sir."

"Thank you for coming here," said Lincoln.

"I didn't really have much choice."

"I suppose not, Ma'am. I'd like to ask you where you were when you saw the men."

"I was on the porch resting in the cool of the evening. The men walked by the foot of the porch. I recognized Arch and I then watched them."

"You are quite certain about Arch. You seem less certain about the identity of the others."

"As I said, I believe one is that man there, but I am not certain. The other man I saw only once and I can not say who he was."

"When the men returned, was there sufficient light for you to see them clearly?"

"It was darker then, but I could see them clearly enough."

"Thank you, Ma'am. I have no further questions for you at this time."

"That didn't help," said Cassandra. "Why didn't Mr. Lincoln question her more closely?"

"She was obviously telling the truth," said Mrs. Myers. "Any additional questioning would make it seem that Mr. Lincoln was not interested in pursuing the truth about what really happened. She admitted that she was not certain of the identity of two of the men. And anyway it is not a crime to go into the woods."

"I call Captain Ransdell to the stand," said Lamborn. Captain Ransdell was an older man with a strict military bearing.

"Captain Ransdell, would you please tell us what you observed on June 1st of this year."

"Yes sir," said Captain Ransdell. "Shortly after dinner, maybe 1:00 or so. I observed William Trailor and Henry Trailor enter the woods at a point to the northwest of town on a little-used road located beyond the main road to the northwest. At some later time, which I estimate to be an hour or more later, I saw the same men come into the street by the butcher's store and then head out of town on the main northwest road which they had passed by before."

"Your witness, Mr. Lincoln."

"Thank you for your testimony, sir," said Lincoln. "I have no questions for you at this time."

"That's it?" asked Captain Ransdell.

"Yes sir," answered Lincoln.

237

"This is not good." Cassandra said to Mrs. Myers.

"No, but there's still no law broken. It's just the appearance that's damaging," said Mrs. Myers.

"I call Dr. Merryman to the stand said." Lamborn.

"Can you describe for us the location and findings of a search you made for me on Wednesday, June 16, of this year?" asked Lamborn.

"Yes sir," said Dr. Merryman. "I was called to investigate a thicket in the brush located in the angle between two roads to the northwest of town fairly close to Spring Creek. I examined the area minutely and located what appeared to be a definite drag trail. It seemed that something roughly the size of a man had been dragged from the thicket to the road. At the end of the drag trail was a distinct set of wheel tracks like those of a small buggy. The tracks of a single horse pulling the buggy were also clear. The trail disappeared into the regular tracks on the road but a similarly clear set of tracks were found where it appeared that a buggy had backed into the edge of the millpond by the dam out there.

"Within the beaten down area of the thicket, I found two triangular human hairs, black in color. These are the type of hairs are not found on the head, but on other parts of the body. It appeared to me that the hairs were cut by a razor so I suspect these are beard hairs."

"Thank you, Doctor," said Lamborn. "Your witness, Mr. Lincoln."

"Good morning, Dr. Merryman.," said Lincoln.

"Good morning, Mr. Lincoln."

"Dr. Merryman, I appreciate the precision in your words. Please correct me if I am wrong but, as I understand it, you said that in the thicket something about the size of a man, but not necessarily a man, was dragged through there. This something could have been a tree trunk or a barrel. We do not know what it was."

"Correct," said Dr. Merryman.

"Also you said that a buggy pulled by a single horse seems to have been at the end of the drag trail at some point. We don't know if the two are connected in any way. The trail might have come first, or the buggy might have come first."

"Right again," said Dr. Merryman.

"You stated the tracks could not be followed." Lincoln.

"Correct. They were perfectly clear in the thicket but then they went onto the road where there were so many tracks that it was not possible to disentangle the one set from all the rest."

"You stated at the millpond there are buggy tracks suggesting that a buggy was backed into the edge of the pond. Some buggy, at some time that might, or might not, have any relation with the other buggy."

"Yes sir. There again the tracks were perfectly undisturbed."

"The two hairs you found are likely to be black beard hairs," said Lincoln. "You can not tell whose hairs they are. You cannot tell us if they were carried there on the wind, or on clothing. You don't know if a black haired man was ever in the thicket." Lincoln.

"Yes, sir."

"Can you tell us when the drag trail was made and the thicket was disturbed?"

"No sir."

"It might have been as early as before the Trailors came to Springfield," Lincoln said.

"Might have been." agreed Dr. Merryman slowly. "I can not aver it was not."

"It might have been made as late as the very morning before the area was searched and long after the Trailors left Springfield."

"Yes sir." agreed Dr. Merryman quickly.

"Likewise with the tracks going into the millpond. They might have been made as early as before the Trailors came to Springfield. Is that correct?'

"I can not swear that they were not made before that time."

"And the tracks could have been made as late as the same morning as the search that found them?"

"Absolutely, Mr. Lincoln."

"Thank you, doctor I have no further questions at this time."

"I think that went well."   Mary Todd leaning well over to talk with Cassandra.

"Mr. Lincoln was wonderful," said Cassandra.

"He was, wasn't he?" asked Mary.

Chapter Twenty Two

Friday, June 18, 1841 Springfield, Illinois

"I call Henry Trailor," said Lamborn.

A murmur of expectation ran through the audience. Henry appeared calm. He was neatly dressed and looked well rested. After he was sworn in, he locked his eyes on the attorney general ignoring the audience and his brothers.

"You are Henry Trailor, brother to William and Arch?" asked Lamborn.

"Yes sir, I am."

"Where do you live?" asked Lamborn.

"In Clary's Grove."

"Did you come to Springfield on May 31st of this year in the company of your brothers and Mr. Archibald Fisher?"

"Yes sir, I did."

"Did you leave with Springfield the following day, June 1st?"

"Yes sir, I did."   .

"When you left, was it in the company of the men you came to Springfield with?" asked Lamborn.

"No sir."

"Why was that?" asked Lamborn.

"One of our number, Mr. Fisher, had been murdered."

Cassandra grabbed Mrs. Myers hand and held it tightly.

"How did you reach that conclusion?" asked Lamborn.

"As William and I were leaving town, he directed me to take a road out of town that did not lead directly to our homes. It was to the northwest but it did not lead to where we needed to go. It was two or three hundred yards to the right of where we should have gone. After we went a few hundred yards into the woods, Arch joined us. He came afoot. William and Arch set me as a sentinel about forty yards away on an unused road to tell them if anyone approached. Then they went to a brush thicket close to where two roads meet. They lifted the body of Mr. Fisher out of the thicket and into the dearborn. They drove off in the direction of the millpond and returned later without the body. They told me that they had taken care of *him*, meaning Mr. Fisher.

"They told me they had killed him the day before and left him in the thicket to hide him. They said William knocked him down with a club and then Arch choked him until he was dead. William directed me to return to Springfield. From there we got on the right road and headed back home."

There was silence in the courtroom.

"Before that point you had no idea that your brothers had murdered Mr. Fisher?" asked Lamborn.

"No idea at all, sir," answered Henry.

"Your witness, Mr. Lincoln."

243

Lincoln engaged in a quiet and brief, but vigorous, discussion with Logan and Baker. The other two lawyers gestured toward Henry, the audience and the jury. Finally, Lincoln stood up slowly and moved toward the witness.

"Good morning, Mr. Trailor."

"Good morning, Mr. Lincoln."

"You understand, sir, that the accusations you make are most serious."

"Yes sir." Henry.

"Except for your testimony, the most serious charge your brothers face is going into the woods. Here in Springfield that's still legal."

"Yes sir."

"Do you wish to change your testimony?"

"No sir."

"How far from your brothers were you when you were acting as a sentry?" asked Lincoln.

"Forty yards."

"Close enough to see if the man you claim your brothers lifted in the buggy was breathing?" asked Lincoln.

"No sir."

"Did you touch the man you claim your brothers lifted in the buggy?" asked Lincoln. "Do you know if his skin felt cold or warm?"

"No sir."

"Nobody in this courtroom, except you, has seen Mr. Fisher alive. Why should we believe what you say?" asked Lamborn.

"Because it's the truth."

"So you say," said Lamborn.

"So I say," said Dr. Gilmore. "It's the truth."

Lincoln recalled Dr. Merryman to the stand. He confirmed that Dr. Gilmore was well known to him as a physician and that they had consulted with each other on medical matters. Dr. Merryman said he had never known his fellow physician to lie. Digby and Baldwin both testified that they had known Dr. Gilmore for many years. They described him as a man of total honesty and impeccable reputation. Baldwin reported that he would trust Dr. Gilmore with his life. Digby said that, upon reflection, when he was seriously ill he had already trusted Dr. Gilmore with his life.

"Your honors," said Lincoln, "the defense rests."

Lavely and May conferred briefly. "Mr. Lamborn," said May, "are you ready to make your closing argument?"

"Yes, sir." Lamborn. He walked over to look at the jurors. Then he spoke. "Gentlemen, do not let yourselves be distracted from your purpose here. You have heard the testimony. William Trailor, Arch Trailor and Archibald Fisher were seen going into the woods together. But only two of them returned. Then they claim that Mr. Fisher has gone missing and they organize a search for him. They organized a series of searches; all of them false. The next day on the way out of Springfield, along a way that does not lead to their homes, William told Henry that he and Arch had killed Mr. Fisher. They clubbed him and strangled him to death. A search of that area showed a tussle ground in a thicket, a drag trail, the tracks of buggy

251

that went from the thicket into the water of the mill pond and black whiskers like Mr. Fisher had. All of these things are physical proof of what Henry Trailor told us. Think about it, gentlemen. Why would Henry lie to the world about what his brothers did? It has to be true. Everything points to it."

"On the other side what is there? The word of one man. Has anyone else seen Mr. Fisher alive? No, of course not. Because he's dead. Would Henry lie and put his brothers at risk? No, of course not. Why did William and Arch claim Mr. Fisher was missing after they took him into the woods and returned without him unless they were covering up for their murder? Can Mr. Lincoln answer these questions? No, of course not. When you return a verdict you must have the courage to put aside the distraction of one confused man and stick to the facts. You must avenge the cruel and bloody murder that is an affront to every decent citizen of this fair community. You must vote guilty."

Lincoln rose to his feet and hooked his thumbs under his suspenders. He walked slowly over to face the jurors. His face was grave.

"Gentlemen of the jury, you just heard Mr. Lamborn pose a number of questions for me to answer. I don't have any intention of answering them. I don't need to. You remember that the defense has no obligation to answer or to prove anything. The prosecution has the obligations. They must prove, to the exclusion of all reasonable doubt, that a crime was committed and that my clients were the ones who committed it. The prosecution in this case has cried bloody murder but they have not found any blood. They have not found a body. One witness, Henry Trailor, saw from a distance of forty feet or so what he describes as a body. He did not ever get closer than that. He says he was told that Mr. Fisher was killed. Another witness, Dr. Gilmore saw Mr. Fisher at his home alive long after Henry saw whatever he saw. Mr. Lamborn described Dr. Gilmore as confused and a horse breeder. You've known confused men. Did he look confused to you? Other witnesses knew Dr. Gilmore. In fact he was known by witnesses called by the prosecution. They described him as a physician, as he himself said, and as an honest man with an impeccable reputation. The prosecution then, wants you to listen to some of their testimony and to disregard the testimony not favorable to their case. I ask you to consider it all. Consider all the testimony of all the witnesses and ask yourselves — Can I exclude all reasonable doubt? I think you can not. I think you must decide that my client is not guilty."

The jurors gathered together briefly without leaving the room.

The foreman gave the verdict, "Not guilty."

Cheers rang out from the audience and people erupted into action. The great majority of the crowd loudly supported the verdict. People pressed forward to shake the hands of William and Arch and to assure them that they had always thought the charge to be ridiculous. In contrast to the celebrants around him, Ignatius Langford sat silent with a sad and shocked expression. He looked as if he had just lost his last friend. Manasseh Porter, on the other hand, seemed elated. He claimed he had never doubted Arch's innocence and had even advised Lincoln as to legal strategy. When asked about the hours of labor he put into the search, Porter replied that he had never so much as lifted a finger in the search.

Asher Keys, the postmaster and tavern owner, came into the church and grabbed Wickersham. He explained that pressing political business had kept him out of town until that very moment. He demanded to know what had happened.

253

"There won't be any hanging," said Wickersham. "Mr. Fisher's still alive. It's a good thing for you that you arrived. I'm about to run your bartender out of town. You can come along and make sure he doesn't rob you blind as he leaves."

"He never could keep his fingers out if the till," said Keys. "But how am I going to find out what happened during the trial?"

"I'll pass the word that you missed the whole trial," said Wickersham. "Your tavern will be packed to the rafters with people who want a willing audience for what they saw and heard."

In their pew the women waited for the crowd to thin.

Mrs. Myers said to Nellie, "This is a good chance for you to talk to Arch. Nobody could criticize you for approaching him right now."

"I just couldn't," said Nellie."

Julia said to Mary, "Are you going to congratulate Mr. Lincoln on the victory? He was magnificent."

Mary said, "In this mob? With everyone watching? I think not, but later on I may ask someone to tell him that I admired his efforts."

"He's never gotten over you, you know," said Julia.

"Do you really think so?" asked Mary.

Maxey shouldered his way through the slowly thinning crowd.

"If you'd like to go to your father and your uncle," he said to Cassandra, "I'd be happy to clear a path for you."

"Thank you," Cassandra said standing up.

Maxey walked beside her toward the people gathered around Lincoln and the Trailors.

On one side Henry, was swearing that Mr. Fisher was dead. On the other side, Arch and William were assuring people that they had harmed no one. They expressed certainty that he would return to Springfield alive.

"I know this is an awkward time," said Maxey, "But if it meets with your approval, I'm thinking of looking for a job in Warren County and I was wondering if I might call on you at your home."

"I approve." Cassandra smiled. "As a matter of fact, in these few days Mrs. Myers has become a dear friend. She's invited me to visit her here. I expect to spend quite a bit of time in Springfield. I've heard a rumor that there may be an job available here at the highest level in the sheriff's office."

"Oh, and I'm happy for the outcome of the trial," said Maxey.

"So am I," said Cassandra.

Elijah Hart, the drayman congratulated Lincoln on his success. Smiling, he added, "You know, it's too *damned* bad, to have so much trouble and no hanging after all."

Two days after the trial ended Dutch Myers brought Archibald Fisher into town. Fisher was alive and nearly recovered. It was only Mr. Fisher's return that which silenced some who still thought the Trailors to be guilty. Henry refused to talk about his testimony against his brothers. Dutch Myers said he regretted missing the "fandango" and that he was sorry he was not able to get back in time to lead the "dead man" into the courtroom during the trail itself. Mr. Lincoln talked little about the trial but he was even more esteemed than before. Mayor Martin lauded the jurors for their sagacity until the town came to see him a man willing to admit his mistakes. Postmaster Keys listened patiently to anyone who would tell him about the trial for as long as they would buy drinks at his tavern. Sheriff Young kept a low profile. Attorney General Lamborn drank and drank until he finally drank himself into a state of stupefaction.

Chapter Twenty Three

Friday, May 1, 1841 Springfield, Illinois

Cassandra was surprised when Elise Myers told her that Abraham Lincoln and James Maxie had come to the Myers house to speak with her. Cassandra hurriedly prepared herself and walked into the parlor with Mrs. Myers.

"Gentlemen, I would like Mrs. Myers to be present while we talk," said Cassandra. "I know I am just a simple country girl but it would not feel proper to meet with two gentlemen without an escort."

"I have no problem with that," said Maxie.

"From what I've heard, you conducted yourself bravely and intelligently when the mob came to call," said Lincoln. "I regret that I have not taken the time to express my admiration for your actions and I would like to do so now, Mrs. Myers. Miss Trailor I think you could not have chosen a better chaperon."

"Fiddlesticks!" exclaimed Mrs. Myers. "Even a field mouse will fight bravely against a hawk if her nest and her family are in danger. I'll hear no more talk about me. I presume you have something that you wish to say to Cassandra."

"We find ourselves in something of a ticklish situation," said Lincoln. "No one better than ourselves is aware of the danger of relying on appearances. What we have to say would not be admissible in a court of laws. We have no proof of our suppositions and even if we did it would not be up to us to seek a legal remedy since we were not the injured parties."

"On the other hand, it would be cruel to keep to ourselves what we now believe to be the reasons and the people that caused your family the ordeal that they went through," said Maxie. "Your father left Springfield immediately after the trial. He said he was done with the matter and bid us not to contact him again. Your uncle Arch…"

"He heard our preamble, and upon hearing that we doubted there was any action he could take to remedy past mistakes he expressed disinterest and sent us in your direction," said Lincoln. "Arch wishes only to continue his life that was so rudely interrupted. In that he may be wise. Henry, of course, still refuses to discuss the trial with anyone."

"Well, I am exceeding curious," admitted Mrs. Myers. "However, it is not my decision. Cassandra, these gentlemen are here to talk to you. Do you want to hear them out?"

"Yes, gentlemen. Please. I want to know what happened, and how it happened. Are there people out to eradicate my entire family? And why?"

"Please bear with us," said Lincoln. "If we answer your questions immediately you might think us deranged. If I may walk with you through our thoughts and actions you may better understand how we reached our hypotheses. One of the greatest gifts of working with Judge Logan, my senior law partner, has been his schooling me on how to put myself in the place of my legal opponent. We now know, as you did all along, that your father did not murder Mr. Fisher. But to others who were in Springfield when the letter arrived there was the appearance that an intelligent and unscrupulous man had used a trip to our city as a means to deprive another of his wealth and of his life. As there was no evidence, no body and no witness it appeared to at least one man that the murderer would escape with no more than rumors and a damaged reputation. That man, at least, was like an ignorant man who finding a telescope put the wrong end to his eye and thought what he saw was accurate.

"The legal case appeared from the outside to be like a strong man standing firm with two legs solidly planted. One leg was the physical evidence. The tussle ground, drag track, and the buggy tracks were one leg. The "confession" was the other. In truth it was more like a tottering scarecrow that might fall with the slightest breeze.

"Part of Mr. Lincoln's problem and part of mine, was that we arrived in Springfield late in the game," said Maxie. "Suddenly everything had to be done at once. And there was precious little time to do it in. I admit some blame in the matter. Sheriff Young had been acting strange. Postmaster Keys was strutting like a Banty rooster. Attorney General Lamborn was giving orders like a general. And Mayor Martin was making speeches about your father's guilt. I should have known something evil was hatching, but I just left as ordered to pick up your father. If I had stayed and investigated my suspicions, you might have been spared your ordeal."

"You are too hard on yourself, Mr. Maxie," said Cassandra. "You found the man whose testimony freed my father and you persuaded him to come with us. You saved my father's life. I will eternally be grateful. And you, Mr. Lincoln, you saved his life in court."

"I agree that Mr. Maxie did well, Miss Trailor, but I did as well for your father as I should have. But I am getting ahead of myself. Although the two legs of evidence seemed to support a strong case, in fact each one was flawy. Consider each one by itself. Could a man be hung because a thicket was trampled, something was dragged, whiskers were found and a buggy left tracks in the area?

On that basis alone – no. Could a man be put to death because one man "confessed" that two other men killed another when the two men denied it and the "confessor's" neck was at risk? Again, on that alone – no."

"But the two together," started Mrs. Myers Myers. "I'm sorry. I did not mean to interrupt."

"That's my point," said Lincoln. "It was awfully convenient that the two were together since neither alone would do. But each is weak and if either fails, the whole fails. Remember a house divided against itself cannot stand. It will fall in on itself. The physical evidence is where I failed your father in the trial."

"But you got Dr. Merryman to admit that it all could have been done at any time from before the Trailors arrived in Springfield right up to just before it was discovered," said Cassandra.

"Much to my shame," said Lincoln. "That is exactly what I did. I held the tool to finish the job right in my hand. I put it away and I did not use it. You remember that Dr. Merryman was a very exact witness. Asked if the tussle ground, the drag track and the buggy tracks could have been made on the very morning they were discovered, without hesitation he said yes. Asked if they could have been made before the Trailors came to Springfield he hesitated and said he could not swear under oath that they had *not* been done as early as that. Those answers are not equivalent. I did not ask the next questions."

"Which were?" asked Mrs. Myers.

"When do you believe that they were made? And then, why do you believe so? After the trial I asked him that. He told me then what he would have said in the trial. He would have said that the thicket had not grown back at all. That is surprising since the supposed murder took place two weeks before the thicket was searched. As a farmer's son with an advanced education in unwanted thickets, I can assure you that if the tussle ground had been made two weeks earlier it would have recovered long before it was discovered. Even more telling was the doctor's observation of the buggy tracks and the tracks of the horse. In the thicket and into the millpond the tracks were perfect. They had not been erased even a little by the wind. They had not been rained upon. No other vehicle tracks passed over them. No animal walked through them between the time they were made and the time they were discovered. Finally, consider that the millpond by its nature rises and falls, slowly but constantly. When the buggy tracks were found they led right into the pond (as if something had been thrown from the buggy backed up just into the pond.) So the height of the pond when the tracks were found had to correspond very closely with the height of the pond when the tracks were made."

Cassandra and Mrs. Myers looked at each other. "Then all that had to be done shortly before the search party arrived," said Cassandra.

"Most likely early the very same morning," said Maxie.

"How positively wicked!" exclaimed Mrs. Myers. "It could only have been arranged to cause grief to your family. Why else would anyone counterfeit a struggle, a dragged body and throwing the body into the pond?"

"Counterfeit?" asked Cassandra.

"It had to be done that day," said Mrs. Myers. "The thicket and the buggy tracks prove it. If the pond had risen and then fallen, the tracks would not lead into the pond. If the pond had only fallen the tracks would not reach the edge of the pond. Perhaps the pond only rose a little. Then the tracks would still lead into it, but then how to explain the thicket? Was there another supposed struggle or another missing person? By now we would have heard of it. And the pond was thoroughly searched. Nothing big enough to require a buggy to transport was found in the pond. So why back a buggy into the edge of the pond and out again if nothing was discarded?"

"That was our reckoning too," said Maxie. "Although we were not as quick at grasping the significance as you were."

"Who made the tussle ground and the tracks?" asked Cassandra.

"We do not know," said Lincoln. "We suppose it to be a small man and not the author of the major plan. There are many men who would act from meanness or curry favor. There are always those ready to join a mob for the excitement if only given an excuse. None of the principals could have done it but any could have had it done."

"This long after the trial whoever did the labor is likely long gone," said Maxie. "I do not expect that we will ever know for certain who did that small piece although I have my suspicions."

"I wonder that you did not question Dr. Merryman before the trial," said Cassandra.

"I had no reason to," said Lincoln. "And I had but little time if I had wanted to. By then I knew your father was innocent. I know Dr. Merryman, Captain Ransdell, and Mrs. Thompson. They are honest citizens. What they said was wholly true which could only help your father. If I questioned them my questions might have encouraged them to embroider their accounts in areas I asked about. The law is best served when witnesses speak the simple truth. Arch did go into the wood with two men. One of them did resemble your father. He bid on a building contract for two farmers. The older farmer preferred to return to his home in stead of returning to Springfield. William and Henry left by one road because Henry wanted to show William the countryside in that direction. Then they came back to town and William started home. As to Dr. Merryman, had I but ears to listen with, I would have known to ask him more questions. Miss Trailor, I am deeply and powerfully ashamed. I beg your forgiveness although I have no right to expect it."

"Mr. Lincoln, I sat in the court room and I listened intently to every word," said Cassandra. "I did not hear it either. Sir, you saved my father's life. I will be in your debt forever. If you feel you need my pardon, I give it to you freely and with great joy. You and Mr. Maxie are my heroes."

"Yes. Yes. How Christian of us all," said Mrs. Myers. "If the physical evidence was counterfeit and it matched the confession. Was that counterfeit too?"

"I yield to Mr. Maxie on that score," said Lincoln. "Once again notice how convenient the two fit together."

"It may surprise you ladies that as a law man I have a distinct distrust in confessions," said Maxie. "I am especially suspicious of a confession that gets the confessor off the hook and impales someone else upon it. Faced with the treat of hanging, a man's word may be less than his bond.

"As to Henry, I reckon he came late to his manhood. He was a wild boy and a handsome boy. The girls admired him. He was able to talk his way out of scrapes where another would have been held to account. William may reckon he was too harsh on his brother but I reckon that his older brothers treated him like a cosset and let him skip out on what others would have had to face. Even so it seemed like he was lately finally becoming a man, marrying, having a child. And on the face of it, it looks bad that he was accused on the 13th and he confessed on the 16th.

"But consider this. From talking with Douglas and Wickersham I know that he was ripped from the bosom of his family. Isolated. Bereft of sleep. Left a starveling. He was struck with fear for his life, for his family, and maybe for his immortal soul. Douglas, Lamborn and Martin went after him in turn. Each could rest while another had at him. Lamborn played the devil. Martin played the angel. They taught him his lines to speak like a player and then they convinced an exhausted, starving and tormented man that he was the author of the lines. If I ever become sheriff, no one in my custody will ever be treated so. Counterfeit? Yes, I would say this was a counterfeit confession. I could not say that even Henry recognizes what happened to him. He may have come to believe what the other, stronger men insisted was the truth."

"And so the second leg of the scarecrow is revealed," said Lincoln. "Coming as they did one on top of the other neither one got the scrutiny that each would have had if they had been found one at a time."

"But who did this and why?" asked Cassandra. "It had to be someone official who could have influenced the search and the who could have gotten to Henry."

"I can not believe it was that popinjay, Postmaster Keys," said Mrs. Myers.

"He is smarter than he looks," said Maxie, "But I know for certain that the others sent him away before the trial started. He may run a tavern but he is not without scruples. It does not reckon that the author of the plan would be away when he was needed most. Keys furthered the plan probably unwittingly. We agree that it was not Keys."

"Sheriff Young for all that he will was willing to close his eyes to what was going on around him, stayed away from the jail while Henry was being questioned," said Lincoln. "That speaks badly of him but it eliminates him as the major suspect."

"Pap Douglas, the jailer, could get at Henry," said Maxie," However, he had no control over the search. That eliminates him as the bull of the herd."

"That leaves us with Mayor Martin and Attorney General Lamborn," said Cassandra.

"They could have been conspirators," said Mrs. Myers

"We concluded that almost certainly to a certain extent both men worked actively to harm the Trailors," said Lincoln. "Both have some amount of blame. However, I still believe that one man was most responsible."

"Who?" asked Cassandra. "And why?"

"As I told you at the beginning, it is my belief that one man seized the wrong end of the telescope," said Lincoln. "I believe, although I can not prove it, that the thought of a clever man getting away with murder was just too much for him. With the trial approaching and no evidence to be found, I believe he decided finally to construct the evidence (or better to have someone construct it for him.) Then he wrote the script and assigned the lines to Henry."

"I see where you are going, but even so it still could have been Mayor Martin," said Mrs. Myers. "I do not trust the man."

"You don't sound convinced," said Maxie. "I know the Mayor used the sunshine to make political hay. I believe he planted seeds and tilled the soil. He benefited from the ruckus and contributed to the evil plan. I doubt we will ever know how deeply he was involved but, I guess like you, Mrs. Myers, I do not believe he was the main architect."

"Attorney General, Lamborn?" asked Cassandra.

"The attorney general," said Lincoln. "He is a man who knows as part of his job that justice in not perfect. Sometimes the guilty go free. So it is likely to be here. Of all the suspects he is the only one who knew exactly what was needed for a murder conviction where there is no body. Lamborn is the only attorney. I imagine that at some point he started to truly believe that your father had cleverly killed Mr. Fisher and to prevent him from getting away with such a heinous crime at the last moment Mr. Lamborn devised a way to have evidence found to "prove" the crime. I do not know how much of the forced confession was planned and how much came from his zealous belief that the guilty were going to escape."

"Wickersham overheard Mr. Martin planning to abandon the search on the day before the confession and the discovery," said Maxie.

"There is that too," admitted Lincoln. "I wonder if having falsified evidence weighed on his conscience and led Mr. Lamborn into the ill-advised way the Trailors were brought into the court. It would have been difficult to find a way to steer more sympathy toward them. He seems to have arranged a verbal cue for a demonstration to break out in the courtroom. Mr. Maxie cleared the agitators out before the session started but Mr. Lamborn acted as if the demonstration might still occur. He had to be able to see that the men he chose were no longer in place. I have tried cases against Mr. Lamborn on many occasions before. No doubt to you he seemed to attack you family head on. From my experience I can tell you that his heart was not in his efforts. He is usually a much more formidable opponent."

"You may not remember that after he lost the trial Mr. Lamborn was gracious and composed," said Maxie. "The day that Mr. Fisher arrived in town, Mr. Lamborn crawled into a bottle and he has not emerged yet."

"What can be done?" asked Mrs. Myers.

"Very little I fear," answered Lincoln. "All we have is speculation and supposition. There is no proof. You could, I suppose, tell people what you believe to be the truth."

"Spread rumor and gossip?" asked Cassandra. "I have been on the receiving end of that too often to take pleasure in turning it on another. No thank you, sir."

"My pardon, Miss Trailor," Lincoln. "I swear that I was not going to recommend that."

"It seems to me that Mr. Lamborn is punishing himself," said Mrs. Myers. "I feel no need to do anything fro my part. Thank you, gentlemen. Learning the results of your inquiries eases my mind. Perhaps you would allow Miss Trailor and me to ponder what you at our leisure."

James Maxie and Abraham Lincoln prepared to leave.

"Oh, Mr. Maxie, I hope you know that I would be willing to act as a chaperone should you decide that you wish to come calling on Miss Trailor," said Mrs. Meyers

"I am very much obliged," answered Maxie.

Chapter Twenty Four

April 26, 1868 Springfield, Illinois

My dearest darling niece, Eppie:

I can not claim that my life can be compared with the excitement that my father had. James Maxie became sheriff at the next election. Mr. Wickersham let it be known that he supported James over Mr. Young and that helped the voters decide. Mayor Martin and Attorney General Lamborn were strangely silent about their preference. Soon after that James honored me by asking for my hand. Over the years we were blessed by God with four children and three of them survived childhood. Jacob and David could not be dissuaded from fighting for the union. I was proud but frightened. If mothers ruled the world there would never be anything as terrible as war. They paid the ultimate price for their bravery. God forgive me, but I believe that James and I suffered more from that than from the gentle death of our darling infant Rebecca. My only surviving child, Mary, wed but she is delicate and I do not expect that she will ever have children. She knows, my dear, how to avoid that risk to her health.

My family hopes I firmly pinned on you, dear girl, and now this family story goes with it. I wish you as much luck with your young man as I have had with James. When a woman marries, she puts her trust in a man to care for her entirely and she sacrifices all her rights to him. Even the poor freed Negroes now have more legal recourse than a woman who marries does (the Negro men at least.)

Yours forever

Aunt Cassandra

Appendix

Historical Notes:

A few days after William and Arch Trailor were acquitted of the murder of Archibald Fisher, a man named Myers returned to Springfield with Archibald Fisher who was still very much alive.

William Trailor did not pay Lincoln's bill of $100.00 for legal services. After William died, about a year after the trial, Lincoln sued his estate and was awarded the $100.00 plus court costs.

Abraham Lincoln and Mary Todd secretly resumed their courtship later in 1841. It is thought that an unknown married woman acted as go between and chaperone. To the surprise of nearly everyone, they were married on November 4, 1842.

Two accounts of the events written by Lincoln

Dear Speed:Springfield, June 19th. 1841

We have had the highest state of excitement here for a week past that our community has ever witnessed; and, although the public feeling is now somewhat alayed, the curious affair which aroused it, is verry far from being, even yet, cleared of mystery. It would take a quire of paper to give you any thing like a full account of it; and I therefore propose a brief outline. The chief personages in the drama, are Archibald Fisher, supposed to be murdered; and Archibald Trailor, Henry Trailor, and William Trailor, supposed to have murdered him. The three Trailors are brothers; the first, Arch: as you know, lives in town; the second, Henry, in Clary's Grove, and the third, Wm., in Warren County; and Fisher, the supposed *murderee*, being without a family, had made his home with William. On saturday evening, being the 29th. of May, Fisher and William came to Henry's in a one horse dearborn, and there staid over sunday; and on monday all three came to Springfield, Henry on horseback, and joined Archibald at Myers' the dutch carpenter. That evening at supper Mr. Fisher was missing, and so the next morning. Some ineffectual search was made for him; and on tuesday at 1 o'clock PM. Wm & Henry started home without him. In a day or so Henry and one or two of his Clary Grove neighbours came back and searched for him again, and advertised his disappearance in the paper. The knowledge of the matter thus far, had not been general; and here it dropped entirely till about the 10th. Inst. when Keys received a letter from the Post Master in Warren stating that Wm. had arrived at home, and was telling a verry mysterious and improbable story about the disappearance of Fisher, which induced the community there to suppose that he had been disposed of unfairly. Key's made this letter public, which imediately set the whole town and adjorning country agog; and so it has continued until yesterday. The mass of the People commenced a systematic search for the dead body, while Wickersham was dispatched to arrest Henry Trailor at the Grove; and Jim Maxey, to Warren to arrest William. On monday last Henry was brought in, and showed an evident inclination to insinuate that he knew Fisher to be dead, and that Arch: & Wm. had killed him. He he guessed the body could be found in Spring Creek between the Beardstown road bridge and Hickoxes mill. Away the People swept like a herd of buffaloes, and cut down the Hickoxes mill dam *nolens volens*, to draw the water out of the pond; and then went up and down, and down and up the creek, fishing and raking, and ducking and diving for two days, and after all, no dead body found. In the mean time a sort of scuffling ground had been found in the brush in the angel or point where the road leading into the woods past the brewery, and the one leading past the brick-yard join. From this scuffle ground, was the sign of something about the size of a man having been dragged to the edge of the thicket, where it joined the track of some small wheeled carriage which was drawn by one horse, as shown by the horse tracks. The carriage tracks led off towards Spring Creek. Near this drag trail, Dr. Merryman found *two hairs*, which after a long scientific examination, he pronounced to be triangular human hairs, which term, he says includes within it, the whiskers, the hairs growing under the arms and on other parts of the body; and he judged that these two were the whiskers, because the ends were cut, showing that they had flourished in the neighborhood of the razor's operations. On thursday last, Jim: Maxey brought in William Trailor from Warren. On the same day Arch: was arrested and put in jail. Yesterday (friday) William was put upon his examining trial before May and Lavely. Archibald and Henry were both present. Lamborn prossecuted and Logan, Baker, and your humble servant, defended. A great many witnesses were introduced an examined; but I shall only mention those whose testimony seemed to be the most important. The first of these were Capt. Ransdell. He swore, that when William and Henry left Springfield for home on the tuesday before mentioned, they did not take the direct route, which, you know, leads by the butcher shop, but that they followed the street North untill they got opposite, or nearly opposite May's new house, after which he could not see them from where he stood; and it was afterwards proven that in about an hour after they started, they came into the street by the butcher's shop from toward the brick yard. Dr. Merryman & others swore to what is before stated about the scuffle-ground, drag-trail. whiskers, and carriage tracks. Henry was then introduced by the prossecution. He swore, that when they started for home, they went out North as Ransdell stated, and turned down West by the brick yard into the woods, and there met Archibald; that they proceeded a small distance further, where he was placed as a sentinel to watch for, and announce the approach of any one that might happen that way; that William and Arch: took the dearborn out of the road a small distance to the edge of the thicket, where they stopped, and he saw them lift the body of a man into it; that they moved off with the carriage in the direction of Hickoxes mill, and he loitered about for something like an hour, when William returned with the carriage, but without Arch: and that they put *him* in a safe place; that they then went some how, he did not know exactly how, into the road close to the brewery, and proceeded on to Clary's Grove. He also stated that sometime during the day, William told him, that he and Arch: had killed Fisher the evening before; that the way they did it was by him (William) knocking him down with a club and Arch: then choking him to death. An old man from Warren, called Dr. Gilmore, was then introduced on the part of the defense. He swore that he had known Fisher for several years; that Fisher had resided at his house a long time at each of two different spells; once while he built a barn for him, and once while he was doctored for some chronic disease; that two or three years ago, Fisher had serious hurt in his head by the bursting of a gun, since which he has been subject to continual bad health, and on occasional abberations of mind. He also stated that on last tuesday, being the same day that Maxey arrested William Trailor, he (the Dr) was from home in the early part of the day, and on his return about 11 o'clock, found Fisher at his house in bed and apparantly verry well; that he asked how he had come from Springfield; that Fisher he had come by Peoria, and also told of several places he had been at not in the direction of Peoria, which showed that he, at the time of speaking, did not know where he had been, or that he had been wandering about in a state of derangement. He further stated that in about two hours he received a note from one of William Trailor's friends, advising him of his arrest, and requesting him to go on to Springfield as a witness, to testify to the state of Fisher's health in former times; that he immediately set off, catching up two of his neighbors, as company, and riding all evening and all night, overtook Maxey & William at Lewistown in Fulton county; that Maxey refusing to discharge Trailor upon his statement, his two neighbors returned, and he came on to Springfield. Some question being made whether the doctor's story was not a fabrication, several acquaintances of his, among whom was the same Post Master who wrote to Key's as before mentioned, were introduced as sort of compurgators, who all swore, that they knew the doctor be of good character for truth and veracity, and generally of good character in every way. Here the testimony ended, and the Trailors were discharged, Arch: and William expressing, both in word and manner their entire confidence that Fisher would be found alive at the doctor's by Galaway, Mallory, and Myers, who a day before had been dispatched for that purpose; while Henry still protested that no power on earth could show Fisher alive. Thus stands the curious affair now. When the doctor's story was first made public, it was amusing to scan and contemplate the countenances, and hear the remarks of those who had been actively engaged in the search for the dead body. Some looked quizical, some melancholly, and some furiously angry. Porter, who had been very active, swore he always knew the man was not dead, and that *he* had not stirred an inch to hunt for him; Langford, who had taken the lead in cutting down Hickoxes mill dam, and wanted to hang Hickox for objecting, looked most awfully wo-begone; he seemed the "*wictim of hunrequited haffection*" as represented in the comic almanic we used to laugh over; and Hart, the little drayman that hauled Molly home once, it was too *damned* bad, to have so much trouble, and no hanging after all.

I commenced this letter on yesterday, since which I received yours of the 13th. I stick to my promise to come to Louisville. Nothing new here except what I have written. I have not seen Sarah since my long trip, and I am going out there as soon as I mail this letter. Yours forever.

The Trailor Murder Case

April 15, 1846

REMARKABLE CASE OF ARREST FOR MURDER

In the year 1841 there resided, at different points in the State of Illinois, three brothers by the name of Trailor. Their Christian names were William, Henry and Archibald. Archibald resided at Springfield, then as now the Sea of Government of the State. He was a sober, retiring and industrious man, of about thirty years of age; a carpenter by trade, and a bachelor, boarding with his partner in business-a Mr. Myers. Henry, a year of two older, was a man of like retiring and industrious habits; had a family and resided with it on a farm at Clary's Grove, about twenty miles distant from Springfield in a North-westerly direction. William, still older, and with similar habits, resided on a farm in Warren county, distant from Springfield something more than a hundred miles in the same North-westerly direction. He was a widower, with several children. In the neighborhood of William's residence, there was, and had been for several years, a man by the name of Fisher, who was somewhat above the age of fifty; had no family, and no settled home; but who boarded and lodged a while here, and a while there, with persons for whom he did little jobs of work. his habits were remarkably economical, so that an impression got about that he had accumulated a considerable amount of money. In the latter part of May in the year mentioned, William formed the purpose of visiting his brothers at Clary's Grove and Springfield; and Fisher, at the time having his temporary residence at his house, resolved to accompany him. they set out together in a buggy with a single horse. On Sunday Evening they reached Henry's residence, and staid over night. On Monday Morning, being the first Monday of June, they started on to Springfield, Henry accompanying them on horse back. They reached town about noon, met Archibald, went with him to his boarding

275

house, and there took up their lodgings for the time they should remain. After dinner, the three Trailors and Fisher left the boarding house in company, for the avowed purpose of spending the evening together in looking about the town. At supper, the Trailors had all returned, but Fisher was missing, and some inquiry was made about him. After supper, the Trailors were out professedly in search of him. One by one they returned, the last coming in after late tea time, and each stating that he had been unable to discover any thing of Fisher. The next day, both before and after breakfast, they went professedly in search again, and returned at noon, still unsuccessful. Dinner again being had, William and Henry expressed a determination to give up their search and return to their homes. This was remonstrated against by some of the boarders about the house, on the ground that Fisher was somewhere in the vicinity, and would be left without any conveyance, as he and William had come in the same buggy. The remonstrance was disregarded, and they departed for their homes respectively. Up to this time the knowledge of Fisher's mysterious disappearance, had spread very little beyond the boarders at Myers', and excited no considerable interest. after the lapse of three or four days, Henry returned to Springfield, for the ostensible purpose of making further search for Fisher. Procuring some of the boarders, he together with then and Archibald, spent another day in ineffectual search, when it was again abandoned, and he returned home. No general interest was yet excited. On the Friday, week after Fisher's disappearance, the Postmaster at Springfield received a letter from the Postmaster nearest William's residence in Warren county, stating that William had returned home without Fisher, and was sating, rather boastfully, that Fisher was dead, and had willed him his money, and that he had got about fifteen hundred dollars by it. The letter further stated that William's story and conduct seemed strange; and desired the Postmaster at Springfield to ascertain and write what was the truth in the matter. the Postmaster at Springfield made the letter public, and at once, excitement became universal and intense. Springfield, at that time had a population of about 3500, with a city organization. The Attorney General of the State resided there. A purpose was forthwith formed to ferret out the mystery, in putting which into execution, the Mayor of the city, and the Attorney General took the lead. To make search for, and if possible, find the body of the man supposed to be murdered, was resolved on as the first step. In pursuance of this men were formed into large parties, and marched abreast in all directions, so as to let no inch of ground in the vicinity, remain unsearched. Examinations were made of cellars, wells, and pits of all descriptions, where it was thought possible the body might be concealed. All the fresh, or tolerably fresh graves at the grave-yard were pried into, and dead horses and dead dogs were disintered, where, in some instances they had been buried by their partial masters. This search, as has appeared, commenced on Friday. It continued until Saturday afternoon without success, when it was determined to dispatch officers to arrest William and Henry at their residences respectively. The officers started on Sunday Morning, meanwhile, the search for the body continued, and rumors got afloat of the Trailors having passed at different times and places, several gold pieces, which were readily supposed to have belonged to Fisher. On Monday, the officers sent for Henry, having arrested him, arrived with him. The Mayor and Attorney Gen'l took charge of him, and set their wits to work to elicit a discovery form him. He denied, and denied, and persisted in denying. They still plied him in every conceivable way, till Wednesday, when, protesting his own innocence, he stated that his brothers, William and Archibald had murdered Fisher; that they had killed him, without his (Henry's) knowledge at the time, and made a temporary concealment of his body; that immediately preceding his and William's departure from Springfield for home, on Tuesday, the day after Fisher's disappearance, William and Archibald communicated the fact to him, and engaged his assistance in making a permanent concealment of the body; that at the time he and William left professedly for home, they did not take the road directly, but meandering their way through the streets, entered the woods at the North West of the city, two or three hundred yards to the right of where the road where they should have traveled entered them; that penetrating the woods a few hundred yards, they halted and Archibald came a somewhat different route, on foot, and joined them; that William and Archibald then stationed him (Henry) on and old and disused road nearby, as a sentinel, to give warning of the approach of any intruder; that William and Archibald then removed the buggy to the edge of a dense bushy thicket, about forty yards distant from his (Henry's) position, where, leaving the buggy, they entered the thicket, and in a few minutes returned with the body and placed it in the buggy; that form his station, he could and did distinctly see that the object placed in the buggy was a dead man, of the general appearance and size of Fisher; that William and Archibald then moved off with the buggy in the direction of Hickox's mill pond, and after an absence of half an hour returned, saying they had put him in a safe place; that Archibald then left for town, and he and William found their way to the road, and made for their homes. At this disclosure, all lingering credulity was broken down, and excitement rose to an almost inconceivable height. Up to this time, the well known character of Archibald had repelled and out down all suspicions as to him. Till then, those who were ready to swear a murder had been committed, were almost as confident that Archibald had had no part in it. But now, he was seized and thrown into jail; and indeed his personal security rendered it by no means objectionable to him. And now came the search for the brush thicket, and the search of the mill pond. The thicket was found, and the buggy tracks at the point indicated. At a point within the thicket the signs of a struggle were discovered, and a trail from thence to the buggy track was traced. In attempting to follow the track of the buggy from the thicket, it was found to proceed in the direction of the mill pond, but could not be traced all the way. At the pond, however, it was found that a buggy had been backed down to, and partially into the water's edge. Search was now to be made in the pond; and it was made in every imaginable way. Hundreds and hundreds were engaged in raking, fishing and draining. After much fruitless effort in this way, on Thursday Morning, the mill dam was cut down, and the water of the pond partially drawn off, and the same processes of search again gone through with. About noon of this day, the officer sent for William, returned having him in custody; and a man calling himself Dr. Gilmore, came in company with them. It seems that the officer arrested William at his own house early in the day on Tuesday, and started to Springfield with him; that after dark awhile, they reached Lewiston in Fulton county, where they stopped for the night; that late in the night this Dr. Gilmore arrived, stating that Fisher was alive at his house; and that he had followed on to give the information, so that William might be released without further trouble; that the officer, distrusting Dr. Gilmore, refused to release William, but brought him on to Springfield, and the Dr. accompanied them. On reaching Springfield, the Dr. re-asserted that Fisher was alive, and at his house. At this the multitude for a time, were utterly confounded. Gilmore's story was communicated to Henry Trailor, who, without faltering, reaffirmed his own story about Fisher's murder. Henry's adherence to his own story was communicated to the crowd, and a once the idea started, and became nearly, if not quite universal that Gilmore was a confederate of the Trailors, and had invented the tale he was telling, to secure their release and escape. Excitement was again at its zenith. About 3 o'clock the same evening, Myers, Archibald's partner, started with a two horse carriage for the purpose of ascertaining whether Fisher was alive, as stated by Gilmore, and if so, of bringing him back to Springfield with him. On a Friday a legal examination was gone into before two Justices, on the charge of murder against William and Archibald. Henry was introduced as a witness by the prosecution, and on oath, re-affirmed his statements, as heretofore detailed; and, at the end of which, he bore a thorough and rigid cross-examination without faltering or exposure. The prosecution also proved by a respectable lady, that on the Monday evening of Fisher's disappearance, she saw Archibald whom she well knew, and

another man whom she did not then know, but whom she believed at
the time of testifying to be William, (then present;) and still another,
answering the description of Fisher, all enter the timber at the North
West of town, (the point indicated by Henry,) and after one or two
hours, saw William and Archibald return without Fisher. Several
other witnesses testified, that on Tuesday, at the time William and
Henry professedly gave up the search for Fisher's body and started
for home, they did not take the road directly, but did go into the
woods as stated by Henry. By others also, it was proved, that since
Fisher's disappearance, William and Archibald had passed rather an
unusual number of gold pieces. The statements heretofore made
about the thicket, the signs of a struggle, the buggy tracks, &c., were
fully proven by numerous witnesses. At this the prosecution rested.
Dr. Gilmore was then introduced by the defendants. He stated that he
resided in Warren county about seven miles distant from William's
residence; that on the morning of William's arrest, he was out from
home and heard of the arrest, and of its being no a charge of the
charge of the murder of Fisher; that on returning to his own house,
he found Fisher there; that Fisher was in very feeble health, and
could give no rational account as to where he had been during his
absence; that he (Gilmore) then started in pursuit of the officer as
before stated, and that he should have taken Fisher with him only
that the state of his health did not permit. Gilmore also stated that he
had known Fisher for several years, and that he had understood he
was subject to temporary derangement of mind, owing to an injury
about the head received in early life. There was about Dr. Gilmore so
much of the air of truth, that his statement prevailed in the minds of
the audience and of the court, and the Trailors were discharged;
although they attempted no explanation of the circumstances proved
by the other witnesses. On the next Monday, Myers arrived in
Springfield bringing with him the now famed Fisher, in full life and
proper person. Thus ended this strange affair; and while it is readily
conceived that a writer if novels could bring a story to a more perfect
climax, it may well be doubted, whether a stranger affair ever really

occurred. Much of the matter remains a mystery to this day. The going into the woods with Fisher, and returning without him, by the Trailors; their going into the woods at the same place the next day, after they professed to have given up the search; the signs of a struggle in the thicket, the buggy tracks at the edge of it; and the location of the thicket and the signs about it, corresponding precisely with Henry's story, are circumstances that have never been explained.

William and Archibald have both died since-William in less than a year, and Archibald in about two years after the supposed murder. Henry is still living but never speaks of the subject.

It is not the object of the writer of this, to enter into the many curious speculations that might be indulged upon the facts of this narrative; yet he can scarcely forbear a remark upon what would, almost certainly have been the fate of William and Archibald, had Fisher not been found alive. It seems he wandered away in mental derangement, and, had he died in this condition, and his body been found in the vicinity, it is difficult to conceive what could have saved the Trailors from the consequence of having murdered him. Or, if he had died, and his body never found, the case against them, would have been quite as bad, for, although it is a principle of law that a conviction for murder shall not be had, unless the body of the deceased be discovered, it is to be remembered, that Henry testified he saw Fisher's dead body.

Made in the USA
San Bernardino, CA
13 April 2015